THE MAYOR'S FIANCÉE

MAIL ORDER BRIDES OF SPRING VALLEY

SUSANNAH CALLOWAY

Tica House
Publishing

Sweet Romance that Delights and Enchants!

PERSONAL WORD FROM THE AUTHOR

Dearest Readers,

Thank you so much for choosing one of my books. I am proud to be a part of the team of writers at Tica House Publishing who work joyfully to bring you stories of hope, faith, courage, and love. Your kind words and loving readership are deeply appreciated.

I would like to personally invite you to sign up for updates and to become part of our **Exclusive Reader Club**—it's completely Free to join! We'd love to welcome you!

Much love,

Susannah Calloway

VISIT HERE to Join our Reader's Club and to Receive Tica House Updates!

https://wesrom.subscribemenow.com/

CONTENTS

CHAPTER 1

Seated uncomfortably straight, her ankles crossed, her polite half-smile stretching her mouth until it ached, Mallory only half-listened to her fiancé's drivel. *He certainly likes the sound of his own voice.* As a choice of husbands, Bradly Newcome would never have been her first. Nor her second. Nor her third. Not that he was bad looking. Plump, going bald, Bradly owned a round, somewhat pleasant face, and his smile charmed many people.

Unfortunately, Mallory wasn't one of them.

"Now I expect you to provide me with sons," he stated, no charm anywhere in evidence. "Strong sons to follow me. You will give me sons, yes?"

"I should hope –"

"Yes, of course you will. As the mayor of our fine town, I'm expected to be a family man. Yes, right. You will attend with me at all social and public gatherings, my dear, and assist me in campaigning for reelection when my term is completed."

"But –"

"You will dress in your finest every day and be a gracious hostess when we host dinner parties."

"Din –"

"I suppose I must allow you to purchase finer gowns." Bradly eyed her best dress with distaste. "Certainly not that rag, my wife wouldn't be seen feeding pigs their slop in a dress like that."

"What –"

"Now onto our home life," Bradly continued smoothly. "You'll receive a small allowance you may spend as you like. I'll also expect you to keep an accounting of all household expenditures. Every penny, mind. In a book. I shall examine it on a daily basis."

"I don't –"

"A pity your family isn't higher in the town's social standing." He pouted. "I need a wife who comes from finer breeding. However, due to your exceptional beauty and grace, you'll make a decent enough wife, I suppose, in the eyes of the townspeople. I do hope your cooking skills are up to snuff, I have no intention of spending funds on a household cook."

Mallory's polite smile faltered at this veiled insult to her parents. "My fath –"

"As our fine town's mayor, I must maintain my high social status. I mustn't be dragged into the gutter by my wife's lack of necessary skills in that regard. You will, of course, be expected to remain polite to friends and enemies alike, smile graciously, protect my reputation at all costs."

All you need do is run your mouth, and you'll ruin your reputation just fine. Soured on the notion of marrying this nitwit, Mallory wondered how he managed to get himself elected in their mid-sized town of Bishop, Massachusetts. Nor did her father give her any choice in whom she married. Just yesterday, he'd approached her with the arrangement.

I've found you the perfect husband, he'd said proudly, *Bradly Newcome, our new mayor. You meet with him tomorrow.*

Mallory craved to slump on the sofa's cushions, to ease her sore back. If her mother caught her slumping in front of not just a guest, but in front of *this* particular guest, she'd never hear the end of it. *I'll wager he'd forbid me to slouch at ease in the privacy of our home.*

"At the same time," Bradly continued his monologue, "I expect you to maintain a sterling reputation. No falsehoods, no speaking to any man without me present, no cursing, certainly no drinking of any alcohol, no gossiping, no displays of temper at any time. Do you understand?"

"I –"

"Good. Now I also expect you to raise the children under these same standards of conduct. You'll treat the wives of the town council with kindness and respect, and you'll head several charities and raise funds for said charities."

Mallory wanted to breathe in sharply and let it out in an explosive sigh. No doubt, her future husband would regard that as an insult. She did draw in a slow lungful of air to ease the restrictive sensations around her chest, and that very nearly ended in a yawn. *Heavens, if I yawn in his face he'll definitely be insulted. Maybe he'll refuse to marry me.* That idea brightened her outlook.

All I need do is yawn –

At that instant, breaking off the potential for insulting her fiancé, the parlor door opened suddenly. Bradly broke off his monologue, and looked around with an annoyed expression as Mallory's mother bustled in. Rebecca's ingratiating smile sat firmly in place, and observing it turned Mallory's stomach. She set a tray of cups, cakes, a pot of tea, sugar, and lemon on the parlor's table.

"I thought you both would enjoy a nice cup of tea," Rebecca stated, her voice both high and shrill. "How do you take your tea, Mr. Newcome?"

"I, er, prefer it plain, thank you." Bradly's annoyance hadn't departed, it appeared, as Rebecca's presence and garrulous nature exceeded his own.

"Our dear Mallory is a fine girl, don't you agree?" Rebecca asked with a high-pitched titter. "She'll make you such an excellent wife, sir."

"Yes, well, I expect –"

"She's a very good cook. Mallory, please don't slouch in front of our esteemed guest. She's ladylike, and very beautiful, our Mallory. We've had many offers for her hand in marriage, but we, her father and I, have had so much trouble in choosing the best candidate."

Mallory half-choked, gulping her tea too quickly at this bald-faced lie. She covered it as both Rebecca and Bradly eyed her in suspicion, hiding her mouth behind her raised cup and forcing back a cough. "Excuse me," she murmured.

"But we feel *you*, Mr. Newcome, are the most deserving of our dear daughter." Rebecca sat, her cup in hand, beaming. "She'll do you proud. You'll never have to hang your head in shame with our Mallory at your side."

"Yes, yes," Bradly answered impatiently. "Now –"

"When is the wedding to be?" Rebecca's eyes widened in innocence. "I must be permitted to invite our dear friends. They would be so angry if they're not invited to attend the nuptials. And we have an extensive family here in the region, so we'd be remiss if they also were not invited."

"Yes, of course, your husband and I will discuss the details."

"I'm so very proud of my dear Mallory." Rebecca turned that ingratiating smile on Mallory. "To have caught the most eligible bachelor in Bishop."

Bradly preened. "Yes, yes, I quite agree with that assessment."

"I will hold my head up high," Rebecca continued, smiling beatifically. "My son-in-law, the *mayor*. All my friends and acquaintances will be so dreadfully impressed. And so very *jealous*, don't you know."

Mallory stared at her mother in consternation. "Mother –"

"Don't interrupt, dear. As I was saying, my social standing shall certainly rise with this marriage." Her mother paused to sip from her cup. "My, my, ladies will seek me out for advice, and they'll certainly invite me to their clubs and sewing circles. Why I do believe I'll become a pillar of our little community." Rebecca beamed.

Horrified, Mallory set her cup aside, and gazed down at her hands, twisted together in her lap. "I don't want this marriage."

"What?" Rebecca asked, her voice rising. "What did you say, dear?"

Mallory stared her squarely in the eye as Bradley gaped, appearing shocked, as though the sofa itself had spoken. "I don't want to marry for your social gain, Mother."

"How dare you say such a thing in front of Mr. Newcome," Rebecca babbled hastily. "I'm so sorry, Mr. Newcome, I don't know what's come over her. She is normally a good child, sweet, and obedient. And *silent*."

"I *never*," Bradly blurted. "I am the mayor of Bishop, woman, and marrying me is the highest of honors. You should be *proud* to marry one such as myself. Why, you couldn't *possibly* marry anyone better."

"I suppose that depends upon whomever I marry," Mallory replied dryly. "A man who loves me for instance?"

"Mallory." Rebecca frantically fanned herself though the room wasn't at all hot. "You apologize this instant. This *instant*. You will marry Mr. Newcome, and you will be a silent, obedient wife. You will do as you are told, your father went to very great lengths to secure this wonderful marriage on your behalf."

Mallory eyed Bradly. He still gaped, his mouth open, and she thought no human being had ever looked sillier. "I apologize."

"There," Rebecca beamed happily. "All is well, then, my Mallory will go through with this marriage, Mr. Newcome. You can count on that."

"It would appear my future bride has some spirit in her." His stiff and unsmiling countenance indicated a spirited wife wasn't what he'd expected. "I shall have to remedy that. I despise women who think they have a mind."

Now Mallory gaped. "Excuse me?"

Ignoring her, Bradly stood. "Thank you for the tea, Mrs. Stewart. I have other appointments this day."

"Let me show you out."

As though Mallory had no more consequence than a lamp, they walked from the parlor together, leaving Mallory in stunned silence. "I can't do this," she muttered, terrified for the first time since her father announced this arranged marriage. "I can't, this is ridiculous, I must tell Father I won't do it."

"You *will* do it, Mallory," Richard said sternly a few hours later. "This marriage is necessary to build our status in this town. Mayor Newcome is a decent man who'll treat you well. Your standing will also grow, I can't see the problem here."

"You can't see –" Mallory choked. "Father, he said he'd beat me."

Richard's eyes narrowed. "That's not illegal. It's quite common for a husband to beat his wife if she displeases him."

"And you beat Mother?"

"Well, no, she's never given me reason to."

"What about what *I* want?" Mallory demanded, outraged at his callous disregard for her safety. "I want to choose my husband, Father. A man who'll love me."

"Don't be ridiculous, daughter." He snorted. "What you want is childish. This man will rise high in this state's politics, you mark me. And as his wife, you'll achieve much status."

"Is that all that matters?" she shouted. "Social status?"

Richard blinked. "Well, of course. I thought you understood that."

"Do you love me, Father?"

"What's that got to do with anything?"

"If you cared at all about your daughter, and her happiness, maybe you'll reconsider this decision."

"Why would I? It's a perfect match, daughter." He sighed, returning to his paper. "I'm not understanding why you're making such a fuss. Do as he says, and he won't beat you."

Dejected and morose, Mallory washed the breakfast dishes a few weeks later, contemplating various means of escaping this fate. Rebecca and Richard sat in the parlor as they usually did, hardly talking. Richard read his papers while Rebecca sewed, each lost in their individual tasks. When the hard pounding came at the door, Mallory, drying her hands, answered it.

"Have you heard?" gasped their neighbor, Jimmy Small.

"Heard what?" Mallory asked, frowning. "Is something wrong?"

"Your folks need to hear this." Mr. Small pushed past her, rudely entering their house without invitation.

Closing the door, Mallory followed him into the parlor where Richard shook his hand and invited him to sit. Standing in the doorway, she listened as Mr. Small spoke eagerly to her parents, not including her in the conversation.

"Mayor Newcome has been arrested," Mr. Small told them. "It's incredible."

"What?" Rebecca gasped, her hand at her throat. "Surely, it's a mistake."

"What can he possibly be charged with?" Richard demanded. "He hasn't done anything wrong."

"That's not what the state's attorney says," Mr. Small replied, twisting his wool cap in his hands. "He goes before the magistrate this morning. Charges of dipping his fingers into the city's coffers. Rumors say he's stolen thousands since taking office."

"That's impossible," Richard stated firmly. "He's an honorable man. I'd never have agreed to marry him to my daughter if he wasn't."

Mr. Small shot Mallory a rapid glance. "You got lucky, Miss Mallory. Marrying him would bring you only trouble."

Mallory smiled. "I know."

CHAPTER 2

"Frank, you need a wife."

Frank gazed dismally at his friend, Sheriff Pete McGuiness. "So everyone tells me."

Pete drank from his mug. "Who else says so besides me?"

"Only every married lady in this one-horse town." Frank gazed gloomily down at his beer. "And marriageable women are scarce in these parts. So just who am I supposed to marry?"

"Good point."

"Ah, well, it's probably best. No decent woman would want to live in this desolate part of Texas." Frank took a long swallow. "Or want to be with me."

Pete scowled. "Why wouldn't a nice, likable lady not want to be married to you? What, you a wife beater?"

"I'd never lay a hand on a woman in anger," Frank retorted. "You know better than that."

"So what's the problem, then?"

Exasperated, Frank sat back in his chair. "I'm a working man, Pete. I have a ranch to run, cattle to raise and sell, branding, you know what I'm talking about."

"So do *all* the fellers round here," Pete snapped. "And they got wives, chillen. They provide food on the table, a roof overhead. You're making excuses."

"That doesn't solve the problem of no women in this part of Texas." Frank signaled the bar's maid for another round. He lowered his voice. "I'm not marrying no tavern wench."

Pete chuckled. "That'll ruin your good reputation right fast."

Tammy, one of the saloon's two barmaids, smiled enticingly at Frank as she set two brimming mugs of beer on the stained wooden table. Frank deftly avoided her gaze and tossed her a few coins. When she sashayed from their table, her hips swinging seductively, he couldn't help but look. He felt his face heat.

"See." Pete slapped his palm on the table. "You're a good-looking son of a gun. Wimmen like you. You got a way with 'em."

"Why ain't you married?" Frank snapped.

"I was once." Pete buried his nose in his mug. "She died. Long time ago."

"I'm sorry, Pete. I forgot."

"Wish I could. Anyways, you're a good man. Too good to not breed, have chillen."

"So we're back to no one to marry."

"You're young," Pete commented. "What, twenty-five?"

"Twenty-six."

"This town ain't gonna stay small forever," Pete declared. "We're on the rail line now. Folks'll pass through here, some will stay, some will pass on. We'll get settlers, too, now that the Comanche been tamed. Where there are settlers, there are wimmen."

"You're optimistic about my chances of getting married." Frank drank from his mug. "I ain't."

"Get your head outta the dang dung pile, boy," Pete snapped. "You pass by, every gal, married or not, turns her head to watch you. I seen it. Give it a year, mebbe two, and you'll find a right sweet gal to marry."

Frank shrugged. "All right."

"You hear 'bout that train got robbed?" Pete asked, shaking his head. "Just last week."

"No, I didn't. What happened?"

"That outlaw gang from up north near Oklahoma Territory. Came south, robbed a train, and killed a bunch of folks."

"Where?" Horrified, Frank absently thought of the hard-earned money in his bank account, and the possibility of losing it all to this gang of thieves and murderers.

"I heard 'bout fifty miles north," Pete replied. "Might come this way, might head west. If them boys're heading for Mexico, they'll pass through here. Keep a sharp watch, son. If'n they're hungry, they'll kill some stock."

"And my place is remote," Frank added, gloomy. "Got only me and ole Mick to guard over five hundred head of cattle."

"Ole Mick fought them Comanche and held his own," Pete added. "Don't be discounting that ole buzzard just yet."

Frank laughed. "He's as tough as old leather, ain't he?"

"That he is. And he can shoot out a feller's eye at three hunnert yards from the back of a running horse."

"So he's told me." Frank drank from his mug. "I ain't seen evidence of it yet."

"Them outlaws come calling, and you will."

"Think the outlaws will come this way?" Frank asked, thinking. "I mean, Spring Valley, Texas ain't got much to attract them."

"I'm guessing they'll head west," Pete replied. "Toward Dallas. Easier pickings that way. But if the federal marshals get wind of 'em, they'll run south, you can count on it. Straight through here to Mexico."

"If that happens, you'll need a posse to run 'em down." Frank grinned. "Not much chance of that happening."

"You and Ole Mick will be my first picks for a posse," Pete grumbled. "Both good shots. Add in Henry Slattery, Mel Pickens, and oh, say, Dan Hartwig, I think we can cause them boys a heap of problems."

Frank nodded thoughtfully. "Could be. Them boys are tough, hard as nails, been with the Confederacy. Fought in the war before settling here. Could be you're right."

"I am right. I might just set y'all up as deputies, just in case. That way, y'all got the law on your side if'n trouble comes. Best be prepared. Them outlaws ride through here, we corral 'em, put 'em in jail till the federal marshals come fer 'em."

"Nothing wrong with being prepared." Frank shrugged. "They ain't headed this way, anyhow. Like you said, they'll head west. There's nothing this way they want."

More than a week after his conversation with Pete in the saloon, Frank rode toward Spring Valley. He'd run out of nails for shingling the barn's roof, an oversight he cursed himself for. He jogged Marlborough along the rutted track toward the small town. The hot Texas summer sun blazed down onto his hat, and hardly a breeze tossed the gelding's mane. They traveled past his grazing herds, munching the thin buffalo grass amid prickly pear growths and thorny mesquite trees.

Frank owned two thousand acres of Texas scrubland after buying other ranches that had fallen into bankruptcy. Banks eager to sell sold him land for the cash he'd inherited from a rather wealthy granddad. And the sales of the yearlings every year kept him both afloat financially and modestly wealthy in his turn.

But running cattle on Texas scrubland was hot, hard, and nearly unrewarding work. Many times, he thought to sell out, and head for greener pastures.

Still, he never did. The harsh landscape called to him, kept him firmly planted in the sandy soil amid the sagebrush and prickly pear.

Dismounting at the hitching post, Frank tied his mount's reins to the hitching post, and rubbed the bay gelding's neck for a moment. "I won't be long," he murmured.

"Morning, Mr. Griffin," called a matron whose name he never could remember. "How are you today?"

Turning toward her, Frank tipped his hat. "Mighty fine, ma'am. And you?"

She tittered, simpering as though she were twenty years younger and not married with nearly grown children. She was certainly old enough to be his mother. "Very well, thank you. You headed for the general store?"

As he'd tied Marlborough to the rail directly in front of Milson's General Merchandise and Dry Goods, that guess wasn't a hard one. "Yes, ma'am."

"Bye, now," she cooed, still simpering.

Embarrassed, Frank nodded, touching his hat's brim. "Ma'am."

Inside the relative coolness of the store, Frank eyed Mr. Milson behind the counter. Dismay filled him as he recognized the only other customer in the place – the very nosy local gossip-monger and all around busy body – Mrs. Barnes. She turned as he walked in, and an almost feral smile crossed her wrinkled face.

"Mr. Griffin," she cooed, her beady eyes bright under her flowered hat. "How nice to see you again."

Frank touched his hat's brim. "Mrs. Barnes."

"We're practically neighbors, dear boy," she purred. "Call me Hilda."

"Um, ma'am. I mean, Hilda." Frank smiled, mortified at how close she stood to him. "How are you this fine day?"

"Quite well, thank you, *Frank*."

His smile wobbled as he turned to Mr. Milson. To his credit, Milson pretended nothing untoward happened in his store, and that a matron old enough to be Frank's mother pressed her hand to his arm. "What do you need today, Frank?"

A face as ugly as an ox's hind end. "Uh, roofing nails. If you have them."

"Sure do. Need a box?"

"Make it two."

"Got it."

Alone with Mrs. Barnes – *call me Hilda* – Frank smiled uncomfortably down at her as Milson departed to the back room. Her hand had not yet left his arm, and remained there, heavy, and unwelcome. But shaking her off, even politely, would be the height of rudeness.

"You need a wife, Frank," she commented, her greedy eyes on his face.

"Uh, sure." He tried a smile. "But they don't come in the mail."

"Of course, they do."

"What?"

Confused, Frank watched as she fumbled with her handbag. She emerged with a small piece of printed paper, her smile radiant. "Take a look."

"I'm not sure –"

"Read it."

The paper was an advert. As Frank read, incredulity filled his mind. "Is this a joke?"

"No, silly man. You can find a wife through the Mail Order Bride Agency. All you need do is write to them, tell them of yourself, and they'll match you with a potential bride."

"I don't believe this."

"Believe it. Many young women in the east cannot find husbands." Mrs. Barnes sighed dramatically, as though such had become a necessary evil. "So the agency matches them with men in the west who need wives. Then they come here, they marry. Happily ever after."

Frank stared. "You mean it?"

"As for the happily ever after part, that's up to you and the lady you choose." Mrs. Barnes shrugged. "It's like an arranged marriage, I suppose. You meet on your wedding day."

"And if she's, er, not nice?" Frank asked. "I'm stuck. Right?"

Mrs. Barnes patted his arm, smiling. "So choose carefully, Frank."

Agonizing over his letter, Frank wrote carefully by the light of the lamp sitting on his rough kitchen table. He explained his situation as best he could, promised to love and cherish, and what he expected of his future wife. *I ain't much, I guess. It's a hard life out here. It's hot in summer, cold in winter. I work hard. But I got a nice house, the roof don't leak. I got lots of cows, lots of land. I swear I'll be a good husband, never lift a hand in anger. I need a wife to tend the house and the garden, raise the kids, wash my clothes. I ain't rich, but I got money in the bank. If you, a kind lady, can accept me as I am, I swear I'll be as good a husband as you need.*

After carefully folding the letter, Frank put it into an envelope, addressed it to the Mail Order Bride Agency, and sealed it. He'd mail it in the morning in town. Sitting back in the chair, he contemplated the far wall. Sure, he had a nice house, he'd built it himself. Three bedrooms, a front sitting room with a large hearth, a broad kitchen, and a root cellar. A loft overhead might make a fine bedroom for the little ones.

He gazed around at the solid walls, the big timbers that constructed them, the adobe that filled the empty spaces between. "It's a fine house," he murmured. "A good start for a family. But what fine woman from the east would want to live in God forsaken, dirtball Texas?"

And what decent woman would want to marry you, fool? Women aren't idiots, as much as we'd like to think they are. No self-respecting gal wants a hard life as a rancher's wife, dealing with the heat, not enough rain, mesquite thorns and doggone armadillos digging up their hard work.

Frank sighed and drank from his glass of cool tea. "No woman with any sense. I'm a fool for even writing this letter. I'll get no reply. And live single to the end of my days."

Still, he mailed the letter the next day. Then tried to forget he ever did.

But when a letter arrived for him on the train a month later, he gaped as he read the words. *If you promise to be a good husband, I'll marry you.*

CHAPTER 3

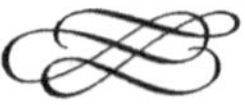

"I didn't pressure him for money." Mallory cried. "Stop treating me like a criminal."

"It's your fault Mr. Newcome is in jail," Rebecca thundered, glowering. "He wouldn't be there if you hadn't become greedy, demanding fancy clothes, jewelry. I heard the truth from Mrs. Howard."

"Answer me this," Mallory snapped, furious at this accusation. "How can I have demanded clothes and jewelry from him when I only met him once? And I told you, Father, *and* Bradly Newcome that I *didn't* want to marry him. You can't blame me for his foolishness."

"Bah." Rebecca snorted. "Why, I can't walk anywhere in this town without the sniggers, the stares. I was to be a fine pillar of this community." Her round face crumpled. "Ladies would have invited me to their clubs, come to me for advice."

"So place the blame where it belongs," Mallory grumbled. "On Bradly's shoulders. Besides, why should our family suffer any social snubs? We didn't have anything to do with his stealing the town's money."

"Our name is associated with his after we announced the marriage," Rebecca replied darkly. "Now people think we were in on it with him. And that's *your* fault."

"Can you hear yourself, Mother?" Mallory demanded. "You and Father arranged this marriage without asking me what I wanted. I told you I didn't want him as my husband. He steals and is caught, and that's *my* fault?"

"Yes, it is."

Throwing her hands up, angry, betrayed by her own parents, Mallory stalked from the parlor. "A sheep has more sense than she does," she muttered under her breath. "What was that passage about casting the first stone?"

Needing to get out of the house, Mallory donned a light shawl, and pinned a small hat to her rich dark hair. Outside, the summer sun beamed down and made her think she should have taken a parasol to shield herself from its rays. *I'm not going to be out for very long, I just want to walk for a bit.*

On the residential street, a few folks passed her by, nodding polite greetings. Of course, the entire town wasn't against her family. Rebecca and Richard simply blew everything way out of proportion. Her confidence rising, Mallory caught sight of her two friends walking ahead of her. Lucy and Susan had both envied her on her engagement.

"Lucy," Mallory called. "Susan, wait for me."

The two young women paused, looking back as Mallory rushed along the sidewalk toward them. Upon closing the distance, Mallory checked her forward momentum, her dismay rising. Neither Susan nor Lucy displayed any sort of welcoming smile, no warmth. And certainly, no friendship.

Stopping, Mallory asked, "What's wrong?"

Lucy and Susan exchanged a quick glance, their expressions nearly identical in their cold neutrality. "What do you want?" Lucy all but snapped harshly.

"I thought to walk with you," Mallory replied, an icy shiver settling into her stomach.

"We don't associate with criminals," Susan stated flatly.

"I'm not a criminal."

"Word around town is that you helped Mayor Newcome steal money," Lucy grated, her blue eyes narrowed. "Stealing the town's money. *Our* money."

"I had nothing to do with it," Mallory protested. "I met the man only once. How can you accuse me on the basis of rumors and hearsay?"

"Because the rumors and hearsay are telling the truth," Lucy snapped. "You're so desperate for a husband, you'd consent to help him steal. You're pathetic, Mallory."

Stiffening, Mallory glared at the women she considered close friends in what now seemed a lifetime ago.

"You don't know what you're talking about," she retorted. "You both know me, and yet you turn against me without asking for my side of the story. You're pathetic, Lucy. You as well, Susan. One day, you'll find yourselves in my shoes, condemned without evidence. And I hope no one has any mercy on you. Just as you have none for me."

Turning, Mallory stalked back the way she'd come, burning with anger, with frustration, with hurt. First her parents turned on her, now her best friends. *Why? Why can't people stop and think? How can rumors suddenly become gospel? If the authorities think I may have committed a crime, why aren't they making inquiries? Why can't people see that if I was guilty, I'd be in jail?*

Tears burned her eyes, but Mallory refused to let them fall. Upon her return to her home, she saw nothing of her parents. Relieved, she wandered into the parlor to sit, staring out the window at the townspeople walking by. *I don't belong here. Not anymore. I've become a pariah, an outcast. There's nothing left for me here.*

"Yet, where can I go?" she murmured. "No family will take me in. Obviously, I have no friends."

Despair and grief filled her, as did genuine fear. "How long before Mother and Father demand I leave their house? Will they throw me into the street with nothing?"

Terribly afraid they'd do that very thing, Mallory rose to pace, unable to sit still. Ideas, one after another, flowed through her mind, all of them worthless in one form or another. Without money, without assistance from her parents, she couldn't simply pack up and leave. She couldn't start a new and fresh life in another town.

"I have so few choices," she murmured, and glanced at the open paper lying on the ottoman. A bold black headline caught her attention. *Wives needed. Husbands await young, eligible ladies.* Picking up the paper to read further, Mallory discovered the advert for the Mail Order Bride Agency. "I write to them and ask them to match me with a husband? How extraordinary."

Hope warred with her fear. Mallory pondered the implications. With nothing left for her in Bishop, why not find a man out west? Men who needed wives, honest, hard-working men are willing to marry a stranger. But could *she* marry a virtual stranger?

"That's exactly what would have happened had he not been caught with his hand in the honey jar."

Sitting down at the writing desk, Mallory wrote her letter. She described herself, her situation, her pleas to the agency to match her with a kind man. Upon sealing it in an envelope, she left the house to mail it.

She then returned home to wait.

In near disbelief, Mallory read the letter from a man in far away Texas, a cattle rancher who desperately wanted a wife. He sounded kind, he promised to never raise his hand in anger; he'd be a good husband. She reread it, then again, a third time.

"Oh, my," she breathed. "This is really real. This man is willing to take a chance on me."

Crossing her bedroom to the window, Mallory gazed down into the quiet street below. All she needed to do was accept his proposal. Board a train that crossed half the country. Meet her new fiancé and marry him. Can she take the chance on him? Was this cattleman as good as his word?

"I have no choice." Helpless, frightened, Mallory recognized her situation as untenable. Her parents had grown cold and distant in the last month. Her mother dropped callous hints regarding how Mallory continued to bring shame to their family. Her father refused to look at her, refused to talk with her.

"They'll be glad I'm gone," she muttered, the pain in that recognition hurt her deep in her heart, a stab wound that might never heal. "They won't miss me."

That hurt made up her mind. Once again, she wrote a letter. A single sentence that would change her future.

If you promise to be a good husband, I'll marry you.

She never told them goodbye.

Her satchels packed, the extra money her fiancé wired her for her travel needs in her handbag, Mallory stepped from her house for the last time. The carriage she'd hired to take her to the train station halted in a jingle of harness and a sharp snort from the horse. The driver leaped down and tipped his cap.

"Ma'am. These yours?"

"Yes. Thank you."

He loaded her possessions into the carriage, then handed her up onto the seat. As he walked around to climb up the other side, Mallory looked at the only home she'd ever known. Somewhere within its depths, Rebecca and Richard had no knowledge their daughter had left them. That they would live the rest of their lives never knowing where she'd gone, or what happened to her.

"You'll never hear from me," she murmured. "Not ever."

"Ma'am?"

"Nothing?" She smiled wryly. "Just talking to myself."

"I do that all the time." He clucked to the horse, setting it out at a quick trot. "The train station, yes?"

"Yes, please."

The carriage rolled through the quiet streets, passing other buggies and carriages, folks walking along the sidewalks. No one paid them any heed. *I'm simply disappearing. Vanishing like a phantom in the night. And no one, no one at all will miss me. Or even care. What a lonely feeling that is.*

At the small yet bustling train station, her driver placed her baggage on the platform as a porter stood nearby. Mallory paid his fee, added a small tip, the most she felt she could afford, and smiled as he tipped his cap politely. "Ma'am."

She showed her ticket to the porter, who nodded, and picked up her satchels. "This way."

Following him, Mallory glimpsed the chuffing monster, smoke billowing from its stack, that would take her to an unimaginable place called Texas. The porter stowed all her luggage, save a small bag with a change of clothes, her toiletries, and books she planned to read on the journey, then showed Mallory her berth. Once again, she parted with a few coins, and entered the tiny room.

Loneliness struck her with all the force of a runaway bull. Mallory sat, her legs shaking, unable to hold her up any longer. Here, on this train, she realized just how alone she truly was. Isolated from family, no friend she could turn to, she sat trembling on her narrow bunk.

"God help me," she whispered. "Let him be kind. Please. Help me to find peace, and happiness and joy with this man. I'm so alone."

The train's sharp whistle startled her. The engine's rumble increased, and her car started to roll slowly forward. Curiosity brought her face to the small window as the train picked up speed. The landscape and the town of Bishop, Massachusetts, passed by outside at an impossibly fast pace.

"There's no going back," she murmured, "I've made my decision. Just as my parents made theirs to turn against me. Do they even know I'm gone?"

Surely by now Rebecca had noticed her daughter wasn't in her room, wasn't in the kitchen preparing breakfast, nor was she reading a book in the parlor. Mallory smiled grimly at the vision of her mother forced to cook for the first time in years.

"Enjoy your life without me, Mother. Goodbye, Father. Sorry, if I can't wish you every happiness in your future."

Drawing in a deep steadying breath, Mallory opened her small bag. The journey to Texas would be a very long one.

Unpacking her belongings in this small room, she hung her best gown on a hook, set her books on a shelf. She removed her shawl and her hat, and also hung them tidily away. Food would be provided in the dining car, as her fiancé generously paid for her meals on board.

Settling in for the trip, Mallory opened a book, and started to read.

CHAPTER 4

His tie strangling him, his frock coat too tight around his shoulders, Frank nervously paced the train station's platform. Ignoring Pete's amused smirks, he untucked his pocket watch for surely the hundredth time and saw only two minutes had passed since the last time he'd checked it.

"You need to calm down," Pete suggested. "The train will be here when it gets here."

"What if she's not very nice?" Frank asked, terrified he'd made a huge mistake in proposing marriage to this lady from Massachusetts. "What if she's uglier than a mud fence? A shrew? I really think this is a very bad idea."

Pete shrugged, his own best frock coat rising and falling, his recently polished boots gleaming under the sunlight. "Make the best of it. You said she sounded very kind in her letter. Ever think she's got the same concerns about you?"

"Yeah." Frank removed his hat, ran his fingers through his hair, then tugged it on again. "She's probably worried *I'm* not very nice."

"And that *she's* marrying a feller who's uglier than a mud fence."

"I wish the train would just get here," Frank muttered, peeking at his watch again. "I'm going crazy."

"Stop that infernal pacing," Pete ordered. "You're wearing them boards right through."

"Is it right that we marry immediately?" Frank's mouth dried at the thought his fiancée may insist upon waiting. *Where will she live if she does? It won't be proper to have her to my place when we're not wed.* "This is a bad idea."

"Too late now." Pete gestured toward the northeast. "There's the train."

Spinning, Frank saw the plume of dark smoke over the low rise, heard the distant chugging of the train's engine. As it was a very small town, Spring Valley's few residents gathered to meet it. Out of curiosity, or eagerly awaiting the mail bag, a crowd gathered nearby. He caught sight of Mrs. Barnes watching him with speculation.

"That nosey old biddy," he muttered.

"C'mon," Pete said. "Let's get to where we can see her get off."

"How will I know her?" Frank complained.

"Son, you'll know her."

Closer to the tracks, Frank watched the train chug around the low hills, and steam toward them. Its whistle pierced the hot air. The screech of metal against metal sent an unwelcome shiver down Frank's back as the engineer applied the brakes.

"This is a bad idea," Frank repeated as the train arrived at a gentle halt.

"Shut up."

A porter leaped down to toss the mail bag to the station master. The crowd pushed their way toward him, leaving Frank and Pete almost alone as people stepped down from the train to stretch their legs and walk around. Amid them, Frank frantically sought a single young lady by herself, yet saw nothing of his bride to be.

Pete elbowed him in the ribs. "Glory," he murmured. "She's a right purty gal."

Suddenly, Frank felt too hot. As though the temperature had climbed another twenty degrees. His tie became uncomfortably tight. Already dry, his mouth had no spit when he licked his lips. "Uh." He managed only the single word.

"You'd best go say hello." Pete gave him a hard push.

The slender young lady in a pale green dress that exactly matched her eyes looked directly at him as he stumbled toward her. She'd piled her dark brown hair under a pretty hat and held a small satchel in her hand. Her face – an almost perfect oval – struck him as the most strikingly lovely face he'd ever seen in his life. Soft lips parted slightly while he paced slowly to her.

"Miss Stewart?"

"Mr. Griffin."

She held out her small hand, smiling a smile that Frank couldn't look away from. It enchanted him and emboldened him to offer a smile of his own, and gently shake her fingers. "It's right nice to meet you, ma'am."

"The pleasure is all mine."

He could easily have stood there all day just looking at her, drinking in her incredible beauty, if Pete hadn't set his hand on Frank's shoulder.

"Ma'am." Pete grinned and took her hand in his gnarled one. "I'm Pete McGuiness, the sheriff around here. Welcome to our little town in Texas."

"Thank you, Mr. McGuiness." Her incredible eyes shifted to Frank and stayed there. A faint blush tinged her cheeks a pinkish shade, and she finally dropped her gaze. "My, er, luggage, it should be here."

"How about I check on that, ma'am."

Embarrassed for standing and staring, Frank's cheeks heated. "I, well, I arranged for us to marry. At the judge's place. Is that all right?"

"It is why I came all this way." Her smile held him utterly in thrall. "Is your ranch very far?"

"Oh. Yeah, well it's a fair piece, I reckon. I brought the wagon, er, for you to ride in. It's just yonder." Helplessly awkward, he gestured toward the buckboard and the patiently waiting mules. "I hope you like me."

Realizing what he'd just blurted without thinking, Frank hastily amended, "You know, my place. My house. It's, uh, nice. I think."

Miss Stewart lowered her eyes and spoke in a voice he barely heard. "I hope you like me as well."

Pete broke into the uncomfortable moment, carrying Miss Stewart's bags. "You two ready to get hitched?"

Miss Stewart nodded. "I suppose I am."

"Come along, then. Frank, close your yapper, you're drawing flies."

With Pete at his side, and the judge's wife at Miss Stewart's, Frank stumbled over his vows. His newly minted wife had little trouble speaking hers, her voice soft yet clear. A petite little thing, her head barely reaching his shoulder, she gazed up into his eyes. And in that moment, Frank realized just how frightened she truly was.

"I now pronounce you man and wife," the judge boomed happily. "Son, kiss your bride and seal the vows."

Bending, Frank planted a firm yet tender kiss on his wife's lips and smiled. "It'll be all right," he whispered.

Gratitude filled her green eyes, her smile. "Thank you."

Pete whooped, and slapped Frank on the back, then kissed Miss Stewart's cheek. "Y'all make a mighty fine couple. You surely do. Now, you take good care of this here gal. You don't, I might have to come out there and beat sense into you."

Frank smiled and offered his arm to his wife. "I plan to."

Frank had no idea how to talk to her.

Behind the sturdy mule team, the buckboard bounced over deep ruts in the track formed by rainwater. Mallory gazed over the broad plains of thin grasses, mesquite, and prickly pear while Frank clucked and whistled to the mules.

"This is so very different from Massachusetts," she ventured after a time.

Here's your perfect opportunity to chat. "Oh?" Frank inwardly cursed himself for sounding like a complete fool. He cleared his throat, but nothing except a harrumph exited.

"New England is green, lush," she murmured, not looking at him. "Thick forests, lots of wildlife. Here, it's so – flat."

"I reckon."

The longer the silences, the more nervous Frank grew. Yet, for the life of him he couldn't untangle his tongue long enough to string a few words together. And the more this continued, the worse it got. Topics of discussion flew through his mind like diving hawks and were gone as quickly.

Mallory suddenly gasped, pointing at the track not far ahead of the mules. "Is that a snake?"

"Yep. Rattler."

The big diamondback slithered into the prickly pear before the mules' hooves trod it into the dirt. Frank felt Mallory staring at him in near accusation, perhaps horrified that he behaved so casually regarding a deadly viper. Still, he could not get his mouth to work, to reassure her that if one saw a rattler first, one usually didn't get bitten.

"Is Texas a dangerous place?" she asked after a very long silence.

Frank shrugged.

After that, Mallory ceased trying to communicate. Flustered, angry with himself, his nervousness growing, he knew he must talk with her. *She's now your wife, fool. You have a lifetime ahead, and if you don't start talking, you'll lose her.* Frank still had nothing he could say, and suspected he made matters terrible for his new bride.

"I – I'm not very good with this," he finally muttered.

"Neither am I."

Frank shot a glance at her face and saw only the back of her head. Needing to apologize, to explain his nervousness, he once again said nothing.

An hour later, he reined the mules in the barnyard, stopping them just short of his veranda. Mick, his aged and tough as nails hired hand, emerged from the barn. Tall and rangy, Mick wore his hat low over his brow, and walked with a slight limp. Frank jumped down from the wagon, aiming to walk around and assist Mallory, but Mick reached her first.

"You must be Miss Mallory," Mick said with a cheerful grin. "Welcome home."

Mallory smiled stiffly. "Is it? My home, that is?"

"I'm Mick." He helped her down to stand on her feet. "And yes, ma'am, this be your home. I help out around here, and if you need ole Frank whipped into line, I'm the man to do it."

Frank caught the expressionless glance she shot him. "Thank you, Mick. If you'll show me where the kitchen is, I'll start supper."

"Come right this way."

Thus, Mick opened the door for her, showed her around the house, made her welcome while Frank lugged her satchels inside. With autumn deepening over the land, the nights became quite cool. As Frank lit a fire in the hearth, Mick sat in the kitchen and regaled Mallory with stories of the Comanche.

I'm making a doggone fool of myself. Staring at her luggage, he decided that perhaps they shouldn't share his bed immediately. Taking them to a spare room further down the hall, Frank set them there, and lit a lamp against the growing darkness. *What is wrong with me? She traveled half the country to marry you, and it's Mick who's nice and you who's making her feel unwanted.*

"Now why would a purty gal such as yourself come so far to marry this young'un?" Mick asked as Frank entered the kitchen.

Mallory eyed him without expression. "I had no choice," she replied simply.

"No decent men out east wanting to marry you?" Mick asked, incredulous.

"I'm sorry if I'm rude," she said, "but I'd rather not talk about it."

Frank tried to help her prepare a beef stew, but she waved him away. Retreating, feeling as low as a snake's belly, he sat at the table with Mick. Being the kind that liked the sound of his own voice, Mick cheerfully filled the kitchen with talk. Nor did he seem to care his audience tended to say very little.

Mallory, as it turned out, was not just a skillful cook, but knew how to look after bachelor males. She served Frank and Mick quickly and efficiently, then sat at the table with her own plate. But Frank noticed she ate very little. Nor did she look at him.

"Eat, miss," Mick urged her. "You're too thin, gal, you need meat on your bones."

"I thought men liked women without meat on their bones," she replied, standing to pick up her still full plate.

Mick sent Frank a hard stare behind her back, his flattened eyes shaming Frank instantly. "I'll, er, I'll clean up," he said, "you cooked."

"It's my job to look after you," Mallory replied tightly. "If you're quite finished, you may leave the table."

Sheepish, Frank half-shrugged as Mick continued to send him that unforgivable glare, his unspoken threat that if Frank didn't mend his ways, Mick would mend them for him. "I – I'll be just out here."

Mick followed him into the front room near the blazing fire, then spun Frank around. "What's that?" Mick hissed. "You're treating that lil gal worse than a tavern wench."

Frank sank to the sofa and put his face in his hands. "I don't know what to do, she's so purty, so fine, I – I just can't talk to her. Everything I try to say just don't come out. I know it's wrong of me, but I can't fix it."

"Boy," Mick growled. "You'd better fix it and right quick."

CHAPTER 5

Mallory slept little that night. After dreading the thought of sharing her husband's bed, then finding herself alone, she had no idea what to make of that. His tense silence, his inability to look at her, his lack of a welcome into his nice house all made her believe he didn't like her. Despite his kindness at their wedding, Frank apparently turned off any and all husbandly feelings.

Tossing and turning, she tried to find comfort in Mick's effusive welcome. *He* at least liked her. And the town's sheriff seemed to have taken a liking to her. But why couldn't Frank? The fact that he didn't want to consummate their marriage told her everything.

She'd made a terrible mistake in coming here.

In the deep darkness of the night, Mallory pulled a pillow into her stomach and wept. Exhausted by the long journey, her nerves stretched taut for far too long, one disappointment and betrayal after another had all taken their tool. Like a broken-hearted child, Mallory wept until she drifted into blessed slumber at last.

She woke to bright rays of sunlight streaming in through the frilly curtains. Her limbs like lead, she crawled into her clothes, and made a half-hearted attempt to brush her hair. Deciding that since her husband refused to look at her anyway, what did it matter if she met him in the morning looking like a trollop?

But Frank wasn't anywhere to be found. The kitchen, warm from the stove and filled with sunlight, was immaculate, yet scented of bacon and fried potatoes. A note sat on the kitchen table. Curious, Mallory lifted it and read: *Mallory, I'm sorry for not being here when you wake up, but I have stock to look after. I'll be home by night. Frank.*

"You can't talk but you can write?" Mallory sniffed yet felt oddly comforted. Frank at least had the decency to reach out, if only halfway. He apologized for not being there for her when she should have been up and cooking his breakfast.

"I don't understand this at all."

Sitting at the table, Mallory contemplated her husband. Far more attractive than she'd ever dreamed, he appeared the strong, masculine cowboy she'd only read about in books.

His sandy blond hair, rugged and powerful features, and straight looking, piercing blue eyes sent a thrill through her every nerve ending, through her heart, the moment they met.

"And it went downhill from there."

With a sigh, Mallory rose to cook herself some breakfast.

The long day by herself ahead of her, Mallory explored her new home. Under the bright sunlight, she wandered amid the barns and outbuildings, kept a careful watch for snakes, but found the scampering lizards a delight. In the biggest barn, she petted the meowing barn cats that rubbed against her skirts, and breathed in the scents of hay, farm animals and manure.

A wide corral held the mules and a few horses munching their hay. One tall brown horse with a black mane and tail ambled to her, obviously curious about her. She stroked its nose, thinking she'd never actually touched a horse before now. In Bishop, she and everyone she knew walked or rode in a carriage wherever they needed to go.

"I expect that in Texas," she mused to the horse busy sniffing her arm, "everyone rides. But I don't know how."

Chickens fled her approach, squawking, while she ambled around the yard, the cats following her like acolytes. She poked her face into a smokehouse scenting of smoke and meat, a tack room filled with saddles and bridles, and a smaller shed where gardening tools were neatly hung on pegs. She discovered the huge garden filled with growing things and realized that was now her task—to keep it weeded and harvest the crops.

"I hope he likes my canning," she commented to the cats, thinking of the root cellar beneath the pantry off the kitchen. She stared at the long rows of corn, squash, potatoes, onions, beans, and beets, suspecting she'd be starting on that garden quite soon. Autumn had now set in.

"A woman's work is never done, eh?" she asked, squatting to pet the cats who'd apparently adopted her as their human.

Back in the house, Mallory cleaned what didn't need cleaning, washed the soiled gown she'd traveled in, unpacked her belongings, and pondered Frank's laundry. But if he needed anything laundered, he hadn't told her. Nor would she venture into his room to search for dirty clothes.

In her explorations of the house, she found that Mick occupied the loft above. Mallory smiled upon remembering his kindness, his stories of fighting the Comanche Indians, how *he'd* made her feel wanted and welcome. Not her husband, Frank. Mick.

"Maybe I married the wrong man."

As the hot afternoon cooled toward evening, Mallory placed a ham in the oven after spicing it the way she'd been taught, cut potatoes into a frying pan, and placed a pot of cut beans onto the stove to simmer. Shortly after nightfall, Frank stepped through the back door.

Dirty, sweaty, his clothes dusty, he looked at her. Mallory met his gaze. For a brief moment, that strange sensation returned to her. That thrill she felt upon meeting him for the first time. That when Frank saw her, he saw her with appreciation, with affection, with the promise of love to come.

Then he shunted his gaze from her. "Smells great," he murmured, lame.

Still, Mallory remembered that look in his bright blue eyes, and wondered.

"Wash up," she said crisply. "Dinner is almost ready."

Over the meal, feeling slightly better than she had the previous night, Mallory once again listened to Mick's tall tales, smiling at his jokes, and felt Frank's eyes on her. But if she turned her face toward him, he stared down at his meal. *He's not shy, I've known shy boys in Bishop. Does he not like me? But the way he looked at me, surely it means something.*

But what that was continued to evade Mallory for quite some time.

A week passed, then two. Her sun bonnet shielding her face from the blistering sun, Mallory harvested the garden. Frank and Mick spent their days doing whatever it was that ranchers do, arriving home late to eat the meal she'd prepared, then sought their beds. She, too, grew weary from toiling under the fierce sun, then shivered in her cold bed after it set.

"Winter's coming," Mick assured her on her second Sunday as a married woman. "We'll be hit with hard rain soon."

Mallory nibbled her lower lip. "I still have so much to do in the garden."

He patted her arm, smiling warmly. "You're a wonderful woman, Mallory. Frank, he has no idea how to be a married fella. In his eyes, you're too perfect, he's not good enough for you."

"That's ridiculous." Mallory snorted.

"His worries, not mine. Just have some patience, gal. He'll come around."

If Frank planned on coming around, he certainly took his time about it. He remained awkward, silent, unable to meet her eyes over the dinner table, which seemed the only time they spent together. By the time she rose in the morning, he and Mick had ridden out. Soon after supper, he sought his room and closed the door.

Late one afternoon, the temperature dropped significantly. Thunderheads boiled on the horizon as Mallory worked to pluck ears of corn from the stalks. Thunder growled ominously as the freshening breeze scented of rain. Keeping a wary eye on the sky, she dropped ear after ear in her basket.

The afternoon darkened into near night. Having seen such storms before, Mallory knew the pounding rain and hail would smash her remaining crops into the mud. Her mouth dry, she frantically tore the ears from the stalks, tossing them into the overfilled basket.

Galloping hooves caught her attention. Riding hard, Frank and Mick charged into the yard. Frank yelled something to her, but the wind carried his words away. Ignoring him, she continued to work, sweating under her shawl despite the cold wind.

"Get in the house." Frank seized her basket, and her arm.

"No," she cried, "I still have time. Let me go."

Wrenching free of him, Mallory peeled the corn from the stalks while blinking away the first drops of icy rain. She had only a single row to finish, then her task was complete. The garden had given up all its goods, and her canning and food preservation would begin.

"That's not worth your life," Frank roared. "That storm can kill. Mallory, come with me."

"No."

Unfortunately, Frank outweighed and out muscled her. Her full basket in one hand, her arm in another, Frank bodily dragged her from the garden. Ears of corn fell to the ground as he hustled her, blinded by the pelting rain, to the ground. Frantic, Mallory sought to pick them up, but Frank's determination overruled her.

In the house's safety, Mallory whirled on him. "I had only a little more to go."

Frank set the basket on the kitchen table. "Do you hear that?" he snapped. "That's hail." He made a circle with his thumb and forefinger. "About that big around. Just one striking your head is enough to kill you."

Flabbergasted that Frank actually spoke complete sentences to her, Mallory gaped. "What about Mick?"

"He'll stay in the barn for now," Frank replied, his anger dissipating. "Once the hail is over, it's just rain."

Mallory gulped, gazing up at the beams that held up the roof. "Will it hold?"

Frank chuckled. "Sure. I built this house to withstand storms like this. It might spring a leak, but I'll fix it."

"The garden will be destroyed."

"Stop worrying about it," Frank said, his blue eyes wide, amused, and looking at her as though truly *seeing* her for the first time. "I know you've worked hard to bring everything in, and I've seen what you've brought in. What's left out there won't matter in the end. We have plenty to see us through till next year."

Nervous, not liking the way the hail pounded the roof, Mallory shivered. "Are you sure it'll hold?"

When Frank stepped to her side, and took her into his arms, Mallory let him. Cold had seeped into her bones, her flesh, and his strong presence, his masculine scent, brought new warmth into them. Her arms around his waist, her cheek resting against his hard chest, she breathed deeply.

And felt safe. And wanted.

"It's going to be just fine," Frank murmured, his chin atop her head. "It's just a storm, and it'll pass soon."

"Are you sure?"

Frank chuckled, his chest vibrating against her skin. "I'm sure."

Thunder cracked, crashing against the house's walls and made the entire house shudder. Brilliant lightning flared outside the windows. Mallory clutched Frank in desperate fear, dreading the moment the roof caved in and buried them both alive. Shivering, terrified, Mallory pushed her face into his shirt, and cried out.

"It's all right." Frank's hand stroked up and down her back, soothing. "It's all right, I'm here, I'll protect you, Mallory. You're safe, I promise."

The terrible pounding of the hail continued, nothing like anything Mallory had experienced back home. In Massachusetts, she'd dealt with thunderstorms, heavy snowfall in winter, the occasional light hail. Nothing at all like this extreme storm that filled her now with terror.

At long last, the hail ceased its assault on the roof. Only heavy rain, lightning and thunder passed over the house. The brilliant flashes of lightning continued to pierce her eyes, but her fear finally fled. Still, she liked being in Frank's arms, and didn't want to move.

The kitchen door opened. Mick's voice boomed over the thunder and his happy grin.

"About doggone time."

CHAPTER 6

Frank stared out at the sheer amount of hail that coated his barnyard the following morning. "Will you look at that."

Mallory joined him on the veranda. "You're right," she murmured. "That storm could kill. What about your cows?"

Frank stared at her wildly. "I don't know. Hopefully, most survived."

"Can they?"

"If they found shelter, yeah." Still, Frank envisioned dead cattle all over his pastures.

"Are cows smart enough to find shelter from storms?"

"Sure, they got good instincts. They'll hide under mesquite trees. But I got more cows than mesquite."

The brilliant morning sunlight warmed the air and melted the ice rapidly, leaving behind a wet, muddy muck in the yard. Mick emerged from the house behind them, yawning while adjusting his suspenders. He put his hand casually on Frank's shoulder, gazing out over the muddy mess even as they did.

"I reckon we'll ride out," he murmured, "check the cattle."

"Yup," Frank replied. "Let's hope we didn't lose too many."

Mallory gazed up at him. "You'll be careful, won't you?"

Liking how she looked at him, her green eyes filled with worry and something else that he couldn't quite identify, Frank smiled. Affection, maybe? A hint of growing love? Whatever it was, it sent a sweet thrill through him and set his stomach to quivering.

"We'll be back late." Frank kissed her soft cheek and recalled her warm lips at their wedding.

The slick mud sucked their horses' hooves as Frank and Mick rode from the barn. The rising moisture from the melting ice mixed with the warm air created enough humidity to make his shirt stick to his back, and oily sweat trickle down the sides of his face. His gelding, Marlborough, sure-footed and solid, carried him to the top of a low hill.

"I don't see anything dead down there," Mick observed, folding his hands on his saddle horn.

Below, brown and white Hereford cattle grazed across the swampy landscape. Frank roughly counted – around fifty munched the wet grass below. "That's right for this bunch. Let's head over yonder."

Riding at a walk or a trot over the slippery terrain, Frank and Mick entered the various pastures that contained his vast herd. In a shallow valley, buzzards flapped and fought over the carcasses of three steers. Frank clicked his tongue in regret.

"I reckon it could be far worse."

"Yep. Them youngsters got caught out," Mick agreed. "The rest are healthy. We got lucky."

Their mounts slipped and slid down hills, clashed against rocks and yet managed to avoid striking prickly pear clumps. Riding amid the thorny mesquite, branches clawed at Frank's shirt and jeans, making him wish he'd donned leather chaps as he usually did for this work. The cows with nursing calves edged away from them as the pair rode within their midst.

"I'm right glad you and the missus are making like man and wife," Mick commented casually. "She's a mighty fine gal."

"She is." Frank eyed him sidelong. "I know I haven't been a proper husband and all. And I'm glad you became her friend."

Mick nodded sagely. "She said once she had no choice but to marry you. What did that mean?"

"She hasn't spoken of it," Frank said slowly, reining Marlborough around clumps of prickly pear. "Just what she said in her letter. That her fiancé was a thief."

"That don't mean she can't find a husband where she's from." Mick frowned. "I reckon there's more to it than that."

"I reckon you're right. Mallory jumped at the chance to marry me, and I ain't all that much. I mean, I don't write well and can't explain myself. She wrote back a single line – I'll marry you if you promise to be a good man."

"Sounds like desperation," Mick mused. "You gonna ask her what's what?"

"Maybe. But that's her business, eh? Mallory might want to keep her past back in the past."

"And what if it's some deep secret that'll come back to haunt her? And you?"

"Really?" Frank snorted. "Can you see Mallory as someone running from the law?"

"That ain't what I meant," Mick protested hotly. "Could be this fiancé might be looking for her. Maybe he's more than a thief. You gotta think she's running from *something*."

"And if she is?" Frank inquired. "So what? Massachusetts is a long way from Texas."

"She got here, didn't she? So can this – whatever it is – she's running from."

"I'll ask her," Frank snapped, irritated. "But if she don't want to talk about it, then that's it. If trouble comes, then it comes."

Wicked storm clouds gathered in the west, lightning flashing deep within their folds. Thunder drifted along the freshening and cold wind. Frank thought to head home before the bad weather struck yet again, but his mind was diverted by Mick's shout from near an arroyo. He trotted Marlborough to the edge and looked down.

A calf bawled amid the scree and rocks, stumbling in its effort to escape Mick's efforts to catch it on foot. His gelding stood quiet, his reins on the ground, awaiting the return of his rider. Frank gazed around for the mother but saw no worried cow anxious for the return of her baby.

He untied his rope. "I'll catch it," he called down.

Twirling the loop over his head, he sent it sailing to settle tidily around the calf's neck. He dallied his end around his saddle horn, then tightened the slack. The bawling calf fought the rope but could no longer escape Mick's hands.

"Easy, youngster," Mick muttered, gripping the bouncing calf around its neck and rump. "You pull, and I'll push."

Together, Frank and Mick drew the young calf up the steep side of the arroyo, Frank backing Marlborough slowly while Mick pushed from behind. Within a few minutes, the calf reached the top of the arroyo and stood on legs that shook. Panting, Mick removed his hat, dragged his hand through his sweaty hair and replaced it.

"No mama?"

"I don't see one." Frank dismounted and examined the trembling infant. "Barely a week old. In good shape, so mama was taking care of him."

Mick gazed around at the area empty of cattle. "She got spooked and abandoned him, I reckon. We'll have to nurse him ourselves."

Frank chuckled. "Think Mallory wants the job?"

"If she falls in love with him, you ain't selling him at the market come fall."

"He's a fine little bull." Frank stroked the soft hide. "Might be we could breed him."

"Hand him up to me."

Mick mounted his gelding, then helped Frank settle the calf across his horse's neck. Helpless in his new position, the calf gazed around with huge, soft eyes, and let loose with the occasional feeling sorry for himself bawl. Frank swung into his saddle.

"That storm's awful close," he commented as the temperature plummeted. "We'd best get home right quick."

The sky swiftly darkened into the shade of late dusk though the sun had recently spoken of mid-afternoon. Thunder cracked over their heads while lightning stabbed down, half-blinding them. Worry filled Frank's mind as he realized just how far they were from the safety of the barn and the solid house. *If we get caught in another hailstorm....*

He didn't let himself complete the thought. Galloping hard for home was out of the question. The slick mud under their mounts' hooves could easily damage or break a leg and send his rider flying. Still, they managed a trot, the calf bouncing up and down on the gelding's neck.

"We'll make it," Mick shouted over the howling wind, holding his hat tightly to his head. "We got no choice. No shelter anywhere."

"I know," Frank yelled. "Let's hope the rain holds off."

The rain, almost in answer to his words, didn't hold off. In lashing buckets and with almost no warning, icy water mixed with sleet slashed their faces. In seconds, Frank was soaked through and shivering. Marlborough lowered his head against the heavy wind and rain, struggling forward with each step.

Mick swore fluently. "This is no good. We got to stop."

"No," Frank yelled. "If there's hail in that, we'll be in trouble."

"We *are* in trouble."

"We can't be that far from home." Frank, like his horse, lowered his face toward his chest and let his hat protect him as much as possible. "It's just yonder over that hill."

"What hill? I don't see no hill. I can't see nothing."

Yet, their horses climbed its slope, struggling through the now thick mud, Marlborough's mane whipping Frank's face. He leaned forward, urging the big gelding on while keeping a close eye on Mick and his horse. Mick reined his gelding in at Marlborough's right flank, the calf's bawling faint under the onslaught of the wind.

At the top of the hill, Frank pointed. "There's the house. See the light?"

"Yeah. Be careful going down. This mud wants to be evil."

"I can feel it."

And he could. Marlborough headed down the hill, his hindquarters slipping through the thick clay, sliding dangerously at times. Leaning back in his saddle, giving the gelding his head, Frank felt his saddle also grow slick. *We're almost there and no hail yet. We'll be fine. Cold, and wet, but fine.*

Reassured by that thought, he peered into the murky rain in an effort to find the trail. He glanced back, saw Mick, the calf and Mick's horse traversing the hill slowly, carefully, edging their way down. Then Marlborough's hooves churned in the slick mud, and suddenly went out from under him in a flash. Frank had no time to react as his big gelding crashed onto his side. Frank's head struck the ground, his left leg caught sharply under Marlborough's heavy weight.

Agony flashed from his leg and lanced upward, meeting the pain from his head. He cried out as his horse thrashed, fighting to get up, smashing his leg further into the mud and rocks.

"Frank!"

Mick's yell coincided with a booming crash of thunder. Lightning stabbed the darkness, and lit Mick's frantic face as he lunged from his saddle. His hooves still unable to catch and hold onto the ground and permit him to rise, Marlborough continued to fight, his struggles grinding Frank's leg seemingly into pieces.

"Whoa," Mick yelled, grabbing the gelding's bridle. "Easy now, easy, that's it, get your doggone feet under you."

Marlborough staggered upright and onto his legs, yet Frank's boot was still caught in the stirrup. Crying out in pain, Frank bent forward to disengage it, then fell flat in the mud, panting heavily. Mick leaned over him, his face in the next lightning flash worried, anxious.

"It is broke?" he demanded. "Your leg, is it broke?

"I," Frank gasped. "I – don't know."

Mick's firm hands ran up and down Frank's left leg, expert and yet painful. Frank yelled for him to stop.

"Come on," Mick shouted over the wind and rain. "Get back on. We can't stay here. We'll freeze to death."

With Mick's help, Frank hopped his way on his good right leg, his arm over Mick's broad shoulders. Balancing delicately on his injured left leg, his hands gripping his saddle, he planted his boot into Mick's strong hands. As Mick heaved, he awkwardly scrambled into his slick and muddy saddle. He gasped for breath, feeling both chilling cold and sweating with heat. He thought he'd vomit at any moment.

"Come on," Mick yelled. "Give him his head, he'll find his way down."

Frank dropped his reins on his horse's neck and gripped the saddle horn with both hands. Sure enough, Marlborough stepped carefully down the hill even as Frank thought he'd pass out. The cold rain slashed his face, blinding him, running down his cheeks and kept him both wide awake and in burning agony.

Marlborough reached level ground. Though Frank did nothing, his horse stopped without warning. Slumped over his horse's neck, Frank heard his name cried out.

But not by Mick.

Turning his head slightly, he discovered Mallory's anxious and wet face close to his. And remembered little else after that.

CHAPTER 7

"His leg ain't broke."

Rain continued to pound the ranch house's roof as Mick sat back, wet, weary and smiling. Mallory wasn't nearly as reassured as he was, since Frank lay on the bed with his face bruised, muddy and still unconscious. "What can you do for him?"

"Get his wet clothes off him," Mick replied. "Get him under covers, stoke the fire. Warm, outta the rain, he'll be all right."

Mallory cupped Frank's cold cheek. "I'm scared he won't be."

"He's tough, lil gal. He's beat up some, but he'll be fine. Help me get him out of these wet things."

Slightly embarrassed to strip her husband's clothes from him, Mallory gritted her teeth and helped Mick undress him.

She tucked the heavy blankets and quilts over Frank's chilled body while Mick stoked the fire in the bedroom's small wood stove.

"I got to care for the horses and feed that calf," Mick stated, rising. "And the stock. You'll be all right?"

Mallory smiled. "I'll be fine."

He set his hand briefly on her shoulder. "I know, gal. You're as tough as he is."

Not feeling as tough as Mick suggested, Mallory watched him leave the room. Under her hand, Frank's face warmed rapidly between the fire and the bed's covers. His skin darkened from the deathly pale shade to a healthier pink, yet when he didn't wake, Mallory fretted. She explored his scalp under his hair and found a lump, crusted with dried blood.

"That's nasty enough," she murmured, rising to fetch warm water and a cloth.

Outside the kitchen window, the storm raged, rain lashing the windows. Even with the stove lit, Mallory shivered with cold as the wind howled around the eaves. Lightning flashed across the dark windows, making her flinch. If the storm planned to add hail into the mix, it hadn't yet arrived.

Mallory cleaned Frank's head wound, then dapped a tincture of iodine to the small gash. Muttering foul words under his breath, Frank's eyes fluttered open as his head rolled from side to side, his mouth grimacing in pain. "That hurts."

"But it'll kill any infection," she replied. "Your head did hit the dirt, you know."

Frank turned his face toward her. A half-smile teased his mouth. "Hullo."

"Hello. Mick says you didn't break your leg." Mallory smiled. "But it's a mess."

"It feels like it. Are the horses all right? The calf?"

"Mick is tending to them now. Just hush. You've a lump on your head, and your leg is swollen and badly bruised. I should fix you something to eat."

Before she stood, Frank caught her hand in his. "You're looking out for me?"

"It's my duty to care for my husband."

"Just your duty?"

Mallory gazed into his blue eyes as they searched hers. "I'd like to make it more," she replied slowly. "If you'll let me."

His fingers tightened on hers. "I've been a rotten husband," he murmured. "Your beauty, your refinement. It scared me. I couldn't talk to you, Mallory. I'm so sorry. Can you forgive me?"

"Only if you drop the beauty and refinement idiocy." Mallory glanced away. "I'm just as scared about this marriage as you are. But I had no choice. Now we're stuck with each other."

"Why didn't you have a choice, Mallory?"

His voice soft, Frank made no demands. But Mallory felt them anyway. Blushing, she replied, "I was engaged to be married." She stared down at her hands. "He was the mayor of my town back home. An important man. My father made the arrangements, my mother found her calling as an up-and-coming society matron. Both thought this marriage would lug them upwards."

"But he was a thief."

Mallory smiled slightly. "He stole funds from the town's treasury. As I'd been named his fiancée, my family shared his guilt."

"That's a load of nonsense," Frank snapped. "It weren't your fault."

"Tell my parents that." Mallory met his gaze again. "Since I was engaged, I carried his blame. My parents, my friends, turned against me. I'd become the town's pariah."

"That ain't right," Frank snapped. "He stole, not you."

"But as he was a prominent citizen, blame must be shared." She smiled thinly. "So when your letter came, I jumped at the chance to escape. Escape my parents, that town, the stares, the condemnation for a crime I never committed."

"Your folks?" Frank asked. "They know where you are?"

"No. I told them nothing. I just left. Boarded the train and never looked back."

"They'll worry, Mallory."

"They'll worry about their social status, not me. Now, I should fix you some soup. You need the nourishment."

Mallory tried to stand, but Frank's surprisingly strong grip didn't allow her to leave his side.

"They ain't worth your spit," he said, his tone low. "You're my wife, Mallory. I'll take care of you from now on."

"Or I'll take care of you." Mallory smiled, then bent to kiss his mouth. "We'll take care of each other."

"I like the sound of that."

The rain slackened as Mallory heated a soup she'd concocted on the stove, yet the darkness outside refused to yield. Lightning continued to flash through the glass window as thunder vibrated the entire house from its foundations. In one such flash, she glimpsed Mick rushing toward the back door.

He closed it against the harsh wind with an effort, dripping wet onto the hard wood floor. Taking off his hat, he shook it, spraying rain everywhere. "Frank?"

"Awake and talking. Get out of those wet clothes before I whop you into next week."

Grinning, Mick shed his hat, his coat, his boots before mincing his way from the kitchen in his stockings. Mallory sighed deeply upon seeing the wet that continued to drip from his clothes, the tracks his socks made on the floor as he hustled from the kitchen and up the stairs. She wiped up the mess with a cloth, then gazed thoughtfully out the window at the darkness and lightning.

"I hope the cattle are all right," she murmured, then chuckled. She'd just taken her first step in becoming a rancher's wife.

Taking a full bowl of soup and hot buttered bread into Frank's room. "This should warm you up," she commented as Frank, wincing with a groan, pushed his pillows against the headboard to lean against it. "How's your leg?"

"I'll tell you," he replied as she set the tray on his lap, "I don't recommend having a horse fall on you. If it hadn't been muddy, he would have smashed it beyond hope."

"How did he fall?" Mallory sat on the chair beside him as Frank spooned soup into his mouth.

"The mud. The soil around here has a lot of clay, and wet clay is slick."

"So it both saved you and caused your injury in the first place." Mallory chuckled. "How's that for irony?"

"I reckon." Frank eagerly devoured her soup and the bread. "Aren't you eating?"

"I will after you finish."

Watching him eat, at long last feeling a connection to Frank – her husband – Mallory's contentment and satisfaction rose. *Are we now truly husband and wife? Is this the beginning of a loving and lasting relationship? Did I truly choose a husband who will love me, and I him?*

His bowl empty, Frank sank back down into a lying position with a sigh. "That was delicious, Mallory. Thank you for looking after me."

She set the tray aside and tucked the covers around him. "I don't mind. I found laudanum in the cabinet. Do you need it for your pain?"

Frank took her hand, his eyes bright with warmth and affection. "I'll tough it out," he answered. "I ain't sure which is worse, my headache or my leg."

Mallory smoothed his hair from his brow. "You need to rest now. Try to sleep, all right?"

"I will."

Bending, she kissed him, a long, tender and lingering kiss to his lips. Frank's hand cupped her cheek, his returning kiss holding a sweet promise of love and romance to come. Mallory smiled as she straightened. "I'll check on you later."

Taking the tray, she blew out the lamp, then left him to rest. In the kitchen, she found Mick, freshly garbed in dry clothes, feeding the fire in the stove. He glanced around as she entered and set the tray on the counter. "How is he?"

"In pain, but good," she answered. "I hope he can sleep."

"He will. That boy can sleep through anything."

Mallory doled soup for the two of them, poured tea, then sat at the table with Mick. He ate several spoonfuls of the soup, then pointed at her with the spoon.

"You're mighty good with nursing," Mick commented. "Can you nurse a calf?"

"I've never done such before," Mallory answered with a giggle. "Is it hard?"

"Nope. Ever milk a cow?"

"Never."

"I reckon I can teach you," he mused, then ate more soup. "Too bad the cow won't accept the little one. Let him suckle on her."

"Poor little thing," Mallory commented. "It must be scared all by itself."

"Nope. Sleeping cozy and with a full tummy, snuggled in straw in the barn. With Frank crippled up, and I got to work the place, that baby needs your help."

"I'll certainly try, Mick."

He smiled. "It's a fine thing to see you and Frank getting along."

"He explained how nervous he felt around me." Mallory picked at her bread. "It's understandable, I suppose. We each married a stranger."

"Your former man was a thief?"

"Yes." Mallory smiled. "The mayor who stole the town's treasury."

"Whoa," Mick breathed.

She briefly explained her arranged marriage, Bradley's arrest, and how her family and friends turned on her. "I needed to get out," she murmured. "Frank's letter arrived at the right time. So I left. Never told my folks goodbye."

"Don't sound like they deserve such," Mick grumbled. "Now you're with us, gal, and starting fresh. You got a new family."

"I sure do," Mallory agreed. "You're more of a father to me than mine ever was."

"Aww, gal, what a kind thing to say. I had me a lil gal once." Mick breathed deeply. "She died before she turned a year old. Caught the influenza."

"Mick, I'm so sorry."

"Wife, too. Ah, well, life is cruel." Mick smiled sadly. "Took to fighting the Comanche after. Never did find the time to marry again."

"You should have." Mallory lightly touched his hand. "You're too good a man to not share your life with a nice woman."

"Here now, you'll have me blushing like a durn milk maid." Mick chuckled. "Quit that."

"You should know I tend to speak my mind."

"And it's a refreshing thing to hear."

The simple meal finished, Mallory heated water on the stove to wash the dishes and tidy the kitchen. After years of cooking and cleaning for her parents, doing the same for Frank and Mick came naturally and easily. Though he usually talked nonstop about his days fighting Indians while she worked, Mick became oddly silent while she cleaned.

"Is everything all right?" she asked at last.

"I just been thinking," Mick replied slowly. "You kids will soon have your own kids. Might be time for this ole geezer to move on."

"No," Mallory snapped, spinning toward him. "You won't go anywhere, Mick, and if you try, I'll drag you back. There'll always be room for you under this roof."

"You mean that, don't you?" Mick seemed amazed at her vehemence.

"I certainly do."

"So you and ole Frank gonna fall in love? Have babies? If you gonna, you might want to consider changing your tactics."

Mallory laughed. "Never you mind. And I think Frank and I are well on our way to falling in love."

CHAPTER 8

Seated on the veranda with his healing leg propped on a stool with a pillow, Frank observed a rider approaching the ranch at an easy canter. The mild autumn weather had dried much of the mud and brought an almost spring-like growth of sweet-smelling grasses and blooming prickly pear. Squinting, Frank stared at the visitor for a time before finally recognizing Pete.

Pete reined in and thumbed his hat back on his head. "Look at you, lolly-gagging in the sun instead of working." He shook his head, leaning his arm on his saddle horn. "Well, you got married and now you think you're the lord of the manor?"

Frank chuckled and pulled his pant leg back to reveal his still swollen and badly bruised left leg. "I got an excuse."

"What happened?" Pete dismounted and tied his reins to the porch railing. He dropped into the chair beside Frank, then sucked in a deep breath. "Mighty fine day."

"Marlborough fell," Frank answered. "During that rainstorm."

"That was a right nasty one at that," Pete agreed. "So where's your lil wife?"

"In the barn. Nursing a calf." Frank chuckled. "Never milked a cow in her life but took to the work like a duckling to water."

"I knew she was a fine gal," Pete commented. "Smarter than you deserve."

"Yep, that's true enough. So what brings you way out here? Just socializing?"

"I wish I was." Pete sighed again. "It seems that outlaw gang's been seen in the area. Killed a couple of ole Taylor's yearlings, stole some horses. I'm aiming to start up a posse and go after 'em."

Frank stared into the distance. "I ain't fit to ride, Pete. Not for a few more days. Mick can ride with you, though."

"I surely need him and his good aim."

"When are you thinking to hunt them down?"

"Dawn tomorrow. I'm glad you can't come along, you need to look after Mallory."

Just as he spoke, Mallory emerged from the barn, then lifted her arm in a wave as she recognized their visitor. Frank watched her stride across the yard toward the house while uneasiness filled his heart. "You're thinking they might be around here."

"Yep. I do. And she can't be left way out here by her lonesome."

"You've got a point there."

"Don't I know it."

"Pete," Mallory exclaimed, climbing the steps onto the veranda. "How nice to see you again."

"And you, Miss Mallory." Pete stood, removing his hat, to kiss her cheek. "Have a sit right there while I lean."

Mallory sat in the chair he'd vacated while Frank studied her lovely profile, her smile. "Pete came to take Mick from us."

"Oh?" Mallory's smile faded as she glanced from Pete to Frank then back. "What's going on?"

"Have a bunch of outlaws that need chasing," Pete explained. "I can't take your useless husband as he needs to stay here with you."

Frank met Mallory's incredulous gaze and shrugged. "Unless I take you someplace safe, I can't leave you alone. Not with them riding around here."

"I can't leave," Mallory said slowly. "I have too much to do. All the canning, the calf, feeding the stock in the barn."

"I done told you your husband is useless." Pete chuckled.

"So Mick will join you in hunting these men down?" she asked.

"I ain't asked him yet, but I'm sure he'll agree to ride along."

"I'm sure I'll be all right," Mallory began, but Frank's raised hand halted her.

"I ain't taking the chance," Frank declared. "These men are bad. They're killers, Mallory. You by yourself –" He shook his head. "They ride here, you're as defenseless as a newborn kitten."

"Even if Frank weren't laid up," Pete added, "I still wouldn't take him on this posse. He needs to be here, looking after you."

Frank plucked her hand from her lap, and kissed it, smiling. "Aren't I the luckiest. I get to stay home with my beautiful lady."

"Useless son of a buck," Pete remarked.

"Go stick your head in a prickly pear patch, you ole coot."

Mallory stood. "It sounds like you gentlemen need some tea to cool your tempers."

She vanished into the house while Pete folded his arms over his chest and stared into the distance. "I hate taking ole Mick from you," he murmured. "You might need him more'n I do."

"You really think they're headed this way?"

"I don't know *where* them boys are headed. It's a bad thing all around having Miss Mallory here and outlaws riding through. You keep a sharp watch out, you hear me?"

"I do."

"Keep a good rifle in your hands, even at the barn. Could be them outlaws are already gone, headed for Mexico. But if they ain't, it's best to be ready for 'em."

Thunder grumbled in the darkness, lightning flickering through the windows. Yet, rain hadn't fallen, nor did the icy wind rise to bandy around the eaves. Her head on his shoulder, both warmly wrapped in a shared quilt, Frank and Mallory lazily watched the fire dance in the hearth.

"What was he like?" Frank asked, breaking the comfortable silence.

"Who?"

"Your fiancé back home."

"Do you really want to talk about him?"

"I'm curious."

Silent for a few moments, Mallory pursed her lips. "He thought me spirited."

Frank chuckled. "Well, he got that right."

"He didn't like spirited women," she went on. "He didn't think women should have a mind to think with."

"That's rather silly of him," he mused. "Why shouldn't a woman think for herself? I happen to like gals who use their heads."

"That's why you're such a wonderful man." Mallory tilted her head back, enabling him to kiss her. "Bradly wasn't such a man."

"Sounds like you escaped a bad marriage."

"I know I did. He treated our coming marriage as though he was buying a horse. I was to give him sons, defend his reputation, be a silent wife who heads charities." Mallory huffed. "Even my folks thought there wasn't anything wrong with him beating me."

"He'd have beat you?"

"He said as much."

Frank growled. "A man isn't a man if he whips either his wife or his horse. And your pa ain't much either if he'd married you to a worthless scum who'd hit you."

"He thought it part of the natural order of things."

"Let's just be grateful for the both of them." Frank grinned into her eyes. "If they hadn't been scum, we'd never have met and got married."

"How very true. I suppose there's a reason for most everything. Right?"

Frank squeezed her more tightly. "Right."

With Mick gone, Mallory took on many of his chores over the next few days. His leg healing, Frank limped around with the help of a cane, carrying his rifle in his free hand. He sat on a stool by the barn door, his rifle across his lap, watching both the area beyond the yard and Mallory holding the bucket of warm milk for the calf.

"You've taken a shine to him," Frank commented.

"I certainly have." Mallory stroked the calf's neck and shoulder. "What should we name him?"

"Cows ain't got names."

"You named your horse," she protested. "I named the cats when you didn't."

Frank eyed the meowing cats circling around Mallory's skirts, begging for their share of the milk. After the calf dreamily lifted his head from the bucket, dribbling white from his muzzle, Mallory tipped milk into a pan.

"There you are, my darlings," she cooed, stroking their backs as they eagerly lapped their treat.

"Next thing you know, you'll be wanting cats in the house."

"What's wrong with that? People have cats as pets where I come from."

"You want that bull in the house, too?"

"We can build him a room off the kitchen," Mallory replied.

Frank gaped until he recognized the humor in her green eyes, the hint of a smile teasing her mouth. "Dang woman," he complained, but couldn't halt his grin. "Too soft-hearted for critters."

"I don't see that as a bad trait," she replied, bending to stroke the cats again. "I want to be kind to all creatures. Even people."

In fascination, Frank watched her steer the calf into a straw-filled stall, then shut the half-door. Inside, the little bull bucked and played in the friskiness of youth and excellent health. Mallory watched him for a time, her face soft, loving, the way he imagined she would look at their own children someday.

"I'll call him Monty," she said.

"Monty? Why?"

Mallory chuckled. "He looks like a Monty."

"Well, one day Monty will be a very big bull, and might decide he doesn't like you anymore."

"You're cynical, Frank," she said, leaning against the barn wall. "Even cattle can remember kindnesses done to them."

Frank eyed the cats, busy washing their faces after their milk meal. "Could be you're right," he mused slowly. "I'd never thought to test a cow's loyalty after hand-raising it."

"Maybe if you had, you'd have discovered he or she was a loving friend."

"After weaning, they were all turned out with the herds," Frank went on. "Heifers were bred, bulls turned into steers, then sent to the markets."

"You won't do that to Monty, will you?" Mallory gazed at him with horror.

"Not if you want to keep him," Frank answered with a chuckle. "But he'll have to earn his keep. Even them dang cats earn their milk."

Mallory gazed down at them in affection as two rubbed against her skirts, their tails high. "I haven't seen a single mouse or rat in here."

"Cats keep the rodents away," Frank agreed. "Protect the grain in them bins, prevent diseases the mice and rats spread. They eat what they catch and look how fat and sassy they are."

Mallory squatted to pet the purring felines, gathering the attention of the others who trotted to her for their share of the affection. She cooed and petted, scratched ears and necks, the cats smacking one another in their efforts to gain all the attention for themselves.

"They sure took a shine to you," Frank observed. "They never did that for Mick or me."

"Because you look at them as objects here to do a job," Mallory murmured. "Not living, sentient creatures. To get love, you have to give love."

"Hmm." Frank glanced around the yard and the surrounding scrubland, then looked back at Mallory. "I had a dog once. Loved that brute till the day he died."

"You should get another." Mallory met his gaze. "Dogs are naturally protective."

"I know. I've been too busy for one reason or another to get one, then give it what it needs. Maybe now that you're here, I'll find a pup."

"I never had a dog," Mallory said with a chuckle. "My mother hated them. Would never permit one in the house. I wanted a kitten when I was small, and she said no nasty little beast would scratch her beloved furniture. She said cats were good for only one thing, and that was dying."

"Your ma sure ain't no good example for a young gal to follow."

Mallory straightened. "She cared only for herself and her social ladder. She left me to my own devices, so I read. And learned from books that kindness wasn't a foul word. And that love, even for dumb creatures, brought peace and harmony to a person's soul."

Amazed at her small speech, Frank grinned. "I reckon I can agree with that. I loved that ole dog, and I 'spect I love Marlborough –"

Mallory's eyes suddenly widened in fear, in horror. "Frank. Behind you."

Rising, Frank spun, lifting his rifle. He caught a rapid glimpse of a bearded and dirty face under a battered hat, teeth bared in a grimace, before the rifle butt slammed into his forehead. He lost consciousness before he hit the ground.

CHAPTER 9

"Frank!"

Mallory lunged for Frank's limp form in the dust, terrified the filthy cowboy had killed him. He lay still, bleeding from a wound over his right eye, but she thought she saw his breath stir the dirt in front of his face. Before she crouched at his side, the man seized her arm and threw her against the barn's wall.

"Don't move," he barked. "I ain't kilt a woman yet, and I ain't wanting to. Stay still now."

Mallory froze, realizing her peril. This cowboy in the grimy shirt and vest with the heavy growth of beard must be one of the outlaws Pete chased. Another, leading two saddled horses from around the side of the barn, eyed her with appraisal, but merely spat a stream of tobacco on the ground.

"Saddle one of them, Bart," the first man ordered, jerking his rifle at the corralled horses. "This here gal is our hostage."

"What do you mean?" Mallory snapped. "I'm not going with you. You hurt my husband."

Bart dropped the sweating horses' reins to the ground, then walked toward the corral.

"Where the saddles kept?" the leader demanded.

Mallory gestured toward a shed. "In there."

"Now you listen good." He stared her hard in her eyes, brandishing his rifle. "Them posse cut us to pieces. It's just Bart and me left. You behave, and we'll cut you loose at the border. Them posse won't dare shoot with you between us."

"You don't know that," Mallory retorted. "They have a sharpshooter with them. He'll kill you before you know he's even aiming his gun."

The man licked his lips, then shot a glance over his shoulder. "He ain't gonna risk killing a purty gal. You're coming with us, missus. Ain't two ways about it."

Half-thinking to resist to the end of her strength, Mallory glanced down at Frank's seemingly lifeless body. "I think I'll decline your invitation."

Before she saw him coming, he pounced on her, seizing her wrists. Mallory fought, screaming in rage, kicking his shins, chopping her free hand at his face, his neck, seeking his eyes with her fingernails. Far stronger than she, he pinned her to the wall with his weight, and quickly bound her wrists together with a leather strap.

Still, that didn't stop her from sinking her teeth into his dirty face, so close to her own.

He yelped in pain, jerking away from her. Mallory fully expected him to strike her for her impertinence, but he wiped blood from his wounded cheek and glared at her. "Bart. Where's that nag?"

"Right here."

Bart led a willing bay forward, then paused to gaze around. "Saddle?"

"Over yonder." The outlaw pointed. "In there."

Turning, Bart led the horse to the shed, then opened the door. In freshly dawning horror, Mallory realized what going with them meant. They intended for her to ride. A *horse*. When she'd never ridden a horse in her life.

"I can't ride," she protested. "Let me stay, tend my husband, I'll misdirect the posse. I promise."

The outlaw laughed. "Sure you will, missus."

"I give you my word," she cried, frantically gazing at Frank. "He's hurt, he needs me. Leave us, and I won't tell them where you went."

"You won't tell cuz you'll be with us. Bart, hurry up with that nag."

Unable to fight with her hands bound together, Mallory tried anyway. She screamed, she kicked, she tried to bite, but the outlaw calmly held her pinned against the wall while watching his partner. When Bart arrived with the saddled horse, they boosted her onto it. And tied her hands to the saddle horn.

"What about him, Dave?" Bart asked, swinging into his saddle.

"Forget him. He'll probably die right there."

Mallory screamed in grief, in rage, in terror. She continued to scream until her throat felt raw, but the outlaws paid her no mind. They spurred their mounts into a gallop, heading south, and led her mount by its lead rope. Having never ridden before, Mallory bounced painfully in the saddle, unable to move in conjunction with the horse. Her screams turned to sobs as the leather strap bit into her skin, the saddle chafed her inner legs.

Fortunately, she'd donned her sun bonnet, thus the sun failed to burn her face. Her hands, however, tied to the saddle, quickly turned bright red. *Get a hold of yourself. Frank isn't dead. Cease your caterwauling. Think. Watch. Listen. Learn.*

Dave and Bart eventually slowed their exhausted mounts to a walk, permitting Mallory to find the stirrups, and balance herself. Keeping her head bowed, she listened intently to their conversation. They spoke in nervous tones of the posse on their trail, of Mexico, of the best way to get there.

"They won't dare shoot with her here," Dave muttered, looking over his shoulder for signs of the posse and scowling at Mallory. "They circle us round, we put a gun to her head. They'll back off, right enough."

Bart gestured southward. "Lot 'o land and little enough water ahead."

"This is ranch land," Dave snapped. "There'll be wells, cattle troughs. We water the horses, keep going."

Her face hidden by her bonnet, Mallory studied the knot that held her to the horse. The sun settled toward the west in brilliant flames of pink, purple and orange. Somewhere to her left, a coyote howled, and was answered by several others. *Under the cover of darkness.*

With slow, subtle movement, Mallory worked the knot. Dave had tied it tightly enough, but Mallory had patience. No horse could run forever, and soon Dave and Bart would be forced to halt and rest them. If she could loosen the leather strap before they halted for the night, she might untie herself and slip into the night before they knew she was gone.

The first part of her plan worked wonderfully. Mallory loosened the knot but kept it tight enough to appear firm. Her second part failed utterly.

Dave hauled her down from the bay's saddle, then dumped her in the gritty dirt as Bart took the horses in hand. "Sit there," he ordered, then stripped the saddlebags from their mounts.

Without letting her out of his sight, he gathered firewood, and lit a small fire where she sat. Dave tossed her a leather bag of dried meat and grain, then a canteen of tepid water. "That's all you'll get, so don't get all whiney."

Mallory drank the water with gratitude, then nibbled the mix. Hard and crunchy, she still found the meal tasty enough. Bart tied the horses to a mesquite tree and sat by the fire for his own dinner. The coyotes yapped and quarreled somewhere beyond the flames' light. Inwardly, Mallory worried about them. She had no idea if coyotes were dangerous or not.

Dave broke out the whiskey bottle. He and Bart passed it back and forth as Mallory lay on the dirt, her arms under her head as a pillow. She listened to them mutter and curse while feigning sleep and waited for them to drop into slumber. Nothing they said to one another indicated they worried she might escape.

Patience. Patience is the key.

Hours passed as she lay quiet, listening to them drink and mutter, throw wood on the fire. Ignoring her many aches, she planned and plotted, pondering just what she would do once Dave and Bart fell asleep. *I have to ride. I have no choice.*

If I walk, they'll track me down and catch me again. Still, she had no idea where to go. In the dark, her sense of direction had dissipated.

If I take Frank's horse, will it know its way home? I heard somewhere that a horse will head home to its stable. I must trust in that.

Her eyes open a mere slit, she studied the outlaws. They'd said they let her go at the border, but could she believe them? The two passed the bottle back and forth, paying her no attention. *If Pete and Mick's posse catch them, Dave will hold a gun to my head. He'll kill me rather than surrender.*

At long last, Dave pillowed his head on his arm, lying beside the dying fire. Bart sat for a while longer, then he, too, covered his face with his filthy hat, and lay on his back. Mallory listened to their deep, rumbling snores, but remained still until their sleep deepened. Hoping and praying the whiskey they'd drunk would prevent them from waking at any small noise, Mallory slowly sat up.

Her eyes on them, she quickly removed the leather strap from her sore wrists. Neither moved, nor did their rhythmic snores alter. Stepping carefully, quietly, Mallory bit her lip and walked away from the fire's light. After pausing to study Dave and Bart for a moment, she headed for the horses tied to a mesquite tree.

Mallory's night vision at its peak, she easily identified Frank's horse amid the three. It had a brown coat while the other two were red, and it was bigger than the others. None of the horses seemed interested in her as she untied the reins and led the horse out from under the tree. Her dread increased as she looked at the saddle high above her.

Please stand still, please don't move, I don't know what I'm doing, but maybe you do. She flashed a quick glance at the fire's glow, and the two dark humps lying next to it. Tossing the reins over the neck as she'd seen Frank and Mick do, she fumbled her left foot into the stirrup as she'd also seen Frank and Mick do.

The horse stood still while she awkwardly climbed into the saddle, and, at last, sat aboard. Mallory tried to relax, to calm her breathing, and shot another look at the fire. Still no movement from the outlaws.

"Get on," she whispered.

The horse swished its tail but made no other movement.

"Giddyap."

Still nothing. Frustrated, scared, fearing she'd make the wrong movement and the horse would either take off running or buck or both, she gripped the saddle horn with both hands. Then she remembered how Frank would nudge the horse with his boots. She tried it, tentative, hesitant, and the horse started out at a slow walk.

Terrified she'd hear the angry shouts from behind her, Mallory squeezed her legs. Her mount picked up speed into a trot, bouncing her around in the big saddle. Gritting her teeth, she endured the torment, and let the animal choose its own path.

"Head for home, big horse," she murmured, glancing over her shoulder at the tiny glowing dot in the distance. "Take us home to Frank."

Exhausted and in agony, Mallory watched the sun rise in the east in brilliant flames of pink and purple. She'd been riding for hours and had no idea where in this vast landscape of scrubland she was. Her throat parched, her fear that she'd die while trying to find her way home haunting the horse's every step, she glanced around for any sign the outlaws pursued her.

She saw nothing except a vast emptiness.

Early morning birds flitted among the mesquite and prickly pear. "The outlaws rode south," she murmured, "toward the border. I want to go north."

The sun rose on her left, thus the horse faithfully carried her northward. She still had no idea where home and Frank lay. She could pass them by and never know it. Despair, terror, and desperation filled her. She'd trusted the horse to take her home, and the beast simply wandered the empty plains without any clue as to where home was.

"I'm going to die out here."

CHAPTER 10

Gritting his teeth against the pain, Frank rode hard and fast. As the outlaws who'd kidnapped Mallory had also stolen Marlborough, he rode his second favorite, a red roan called Samson. The three horses created tracks in the gritty dirt he followed easily, and while they gave their horses a breather, he dared not spare Samson.

Not while Mallory's life depended upon his catching up to her.

The trail led straight southward, unvarying, and plain to see. At dusk, he slowed his frantic pace, easing Samson to a walk as he studied the ground, recognizing Marlborough's hoof prints among the others. "I see your beasts are near exhaustion," he muttered. "You'll have to stop for the night, won't you?"

Breathing heavily, Samson suddenly whipped his head up and toward the east, his ears perked forward. Frank seized his rifle from its scabbard, cocking it, seeing what his horse saw. A plume of dust that only a band of galloping horses could create.

And they headed straight for him.

While he doubted the outlaws had circled around to outflank him, Frank trotted Samson around the far side of a thick growth of mesquite and waited. After a short while, the group of cantering horses drew close enough for Frank to observe the riders' faces.

He sucked in a deep breath.

"Frank," Mick yelled, "where you at?"

"Here."

Frank guided his roan from around the big thicket, and trotted to meet Mick, Pete with Henry Slattery, Mel Pickens, and grouchy Dan Hartwig. Mick's and Pete's expressions registered their concern upon seeing the dried blood still on Frank's brow and cheek.

"What happened?" Pete demanded.

"Two outlaws hit my place," Frank answered, terse, gesturing southward. "Took Mallory, I'm following their tracks now."

"Let's go," Pete ordered, reining his gelding around. "We'll talk as we ride."

The group thundered at a fast gallop along the outlaws' trail as Frank briefly explained getting struck in the head, and, upon waking, found Mallory and Marlborough gone. "My horse is almost played out, but theirs are, too."

"We'll follow as best we can through the night," Pete said grimly. "They'll have to stop and rest their horses."

"How'd you find me?" Frank asked, eyeing Mick at his side.

"Pete spotted you," he answered. "Saw dust, took a peek. Recognized you right away."

"We kilt the other bandits," Mel Pickens stated, spitting tobacco on the ground even as he rode at a gallop. "Two got away. Them's the ones got yer missus."

Frank tried to shy away from thoughts of what might be happening to Mallory at that very moment. *Once they stop, what will they do? If they so much as touch her....* His mind winced at imagining Mallory's screams, the outlaws tormenting her.

"She'll be all right," Mick said as though reading Frank's mind. "They want her as a hostage. That's why they took her."

Frank licked his dry lips with an even drier tongue. "How can you be sure?"

"They're desperate," Pete answered for him. "They only escaped by the hair on their heads. With her, they know Mick here won't risk shooting them through the eyes."

The sun slid over the horizon in a blaze of fiery orange, red and purple flames, the fresh nightfall hindered their ability to follow the trail. Frank forced back his despair as Pete slowed their pace from a lope to a trot, studying the earth beneath him intently. For more than an hour they rode as the stars gleamed overhead.

"We'll lose them in the dark," Frank snapped. "What if they turn aside?"

"Shush," Pete hissed, staring intently southward. "All of you, be quiet."

Pete reined in to a halt, his raised hand halting his posse. Plucking a spyglass from his saddlebags, he peered through it. Taking deep breaths to calm himself, Frank waited, trying to see what had caught Pete's attention.

"There's a fire yonder," Pete said, lowering his glasses. "It's got to be them."

"Let's ride then," Frank grated, lifting his reins.

Pete grabbed Samson's bridle. "We make a plan first, dang it. Go at them quiet like. We ride in half-cocked, them boys'll use Mallory as their hostage. We gotta take 'em by surprise."

Frank relented. "What's your plan?"

"This."

Pete rapidly issued orders. Paired with Mick, Frank rode slightly to the east while the others vanished into the darkness. Coyotes yapped from somewhere nearby, and a deer leaped from hiding to race away from the danger they posed. The light of the campfire drew Frank and Mick, yet Frank heard nothing over the soft sough of the wind. No voices, no screams, no bellow of anger.

"It's awful quiet over yonder," Mick murmured. "Could be they're asleep?"

Frank pulled his rifle from its scabbard. "Let's hope so."

His heart pounding, he rode at a walk toward the fire. As he drew closer, he saw few flames and only coals glowing in the night. And the two shapes lying beside it. *Where's Mallory?* Frantic with terror, he saw nothing of her within the fire's circle of light.

A single gunshot ripped through the darkness.

Pete's signal.

Frank and Mick kicked their horses into a gallop, their rifles aimed at the two dark figures scrambling to their feet. Before they reached their tied horses, the outlaws cried out in fear, raising their hands in surrender. Pete and Mel charged into their path, effectively blocking them in. Henry and Dan rode in from the side even as Frank and Mick pushed their mounts into the firelight.

"Don't kill us," cried one. "We surrender, don't shoot."

Frank leaped from his saddle, searching for any sign of Mallory. His rage rose upon finding only a flattened spot in the dirt not far from the fire. He slammed the butt of his gun into the outlaw's gut, sending him, breathless, to the ground.

"Where is she?" he roared, aiming his rifle into the terrified man's face. "What did you do to my wife?"

"She – she was here," the other stammered. "We didn't touch her, I swear. She – she must've run off."

Mick rode between Frank and his victim. "Frank, there's only two horses here. Mallory escaped."

Pete also dismounted, as did the others. He kicked the groaning man on the ground onto his face and yanked his arms behind his back. Now manacled, the man lay gasping and helpless in the dirt. Mel handed him a second pair, and Pete quickly apprehended the second outlaw.

His worry only increasing with Mallory gone, Frank stabbed a long heavy branch into the fire. Once it caught, he used it as a torch to search the ground near the tied horses. Sure enough, Marlborough's tracks led somewhat north and east.

Toward home.

"We ride."

Vaulting into his saddle, he reined Samson northeast. Mick followed as Frank kicked the roan into yet another ground eating gallop.

"She doesn't know how to ride," Frank growled. "What if she falls off? Hits her head?"

"Don't give in to fear," Mick ordered. "Mallory has sense. She'll ride slow. Hang on, look. That horse of yours looks like he's headed home."

Frank expelled a sharp gust of air. "Marlborough *knows* she's not in control. He'll head home, you're right."

"If she's riding slow, we don't have to kill our horses catching up." Mick reined to a swift trot.

Frank followed suit, feeling his confidence rise, his faith in his sensible horse filling his heart. "He's got a good head on him," he said quickly. "He'll look after her."

Both horses stumbled in weariness, their heads hanging low, as the dawn emerged in the east. Frank, ignoring his own pain and exhaustion, scanned the steadily lightening horizon to the north. "I wish I'd thought to borrow Pete's spyglass," he muttered.

Mick leaned out of his saddle to study the ground. "I'm not seeing tracks."

Fear stabbed through Frank. "Where can she be? Did she head in another direction?"

"Unlikely," Mick replied. "We're probably riding parallel to her trail."

"We should have caught up to her by now."

"Easy," Mick ordered. "If she's on that horse, we'll find her."

And what if she's not on the horse? And we passed her body by in the dark? Frank refused to give tongue to his panicked thought. *She has to be on him, she has to be.*

Mick stabbed a finger over his mount's head. "There. A horse."

Frank didn't try to see for himself. He kicked Samson into a gallop, forcing the gelding into a pace he couldn't hold for very long. *I'll kill him if I have to as long as I find Mallory.* The dark figure on the bleak horizon grew in size and shape – and the horse had a rider.

"It's Mallory."

It soon grew clear Mallory had seen them as well. But rather than wait, she urged Marlborough into a canter, riding away from them. Dismayed, Frank knew Samson could never catch up to the fresher Marlborough.

"She thinks we're the outlaws," Mick snapped, lashing his gelding with his reins. "She's running."

"Mallory!" Frank screamed, but knew she rode too far away to hear him.

Samson's neck foamed with sweat, his nostrils flared as he gasped for breath, and fought to maintain his gallop. Frank knew Mick's horse was just as exhausted and feared they'd both collapse under them while Mallory rode away, never knowing Frank pursued her.

"We're catching up," Mick crowed. "Hang tough."

Sure enough, Frank realized they'd closed the distance. Mallory rode at a lope, her body flopping in the saddle while Marlborough appeared ready to call a halt despite her urging. *Stop, son, stop. Turn around, let her recognize us.*

Mallory shot a frantic glance over her shoulder but didn't slow.

"Come on, Samson," Frank groaned, "don't die on me now."

"Mallory!" Mick shouted. "Mallory, stop, it's us."

She still didn't rein in or turn around. Frank joined his voice to Mick's, yelling Mallory's name over and over. Surely, they were close enough for her to hear their shouts. Or perhaps she heard them but didn't hear her name in the voices behind her.

"Mallory!"

Samson stumbled, his nose striking the dirt, and flipped onto his back. Frank leaped from the saddle before the big gelding rolled over him and hit the ground on his shoulder. Gasping, dirt in his eyes, his nose, his mouth, he half-saw Mick rein around to help him.

"Mallory," he groaned, fighting his way to his feet just as Samson staggered up.

"Frank!"

Frank swiped dirt from his eyes, blinking, disbelieving. Marlborough cantered toward them, not away. "Mallory!"

Laughing, crying, Mallory did little to halt Marlborough upon reaching them, but he stopped at Frank. Mallory flung herself from his saddle and launched herself into his arms.

"Oh, Frank, Frank," she wept within the circle of his arms. "I thought you were those bad men chasing me."

Frank stroked her hair down her back, muttering, "It's all right, you're safe, it's all right, you're safe."

Mallory lifted her tear-streaked face to his, her smile wobbling. "You're all right."

Frank chuckled and kissed her. "So are you."

"I love you," Mallory told him through her tears. "I love you. I love you so much."

Frank caressed her cheek. "I love you, my beautiful wife."

"Good," Mick grumbled from behind Frank. "We got that out of the way. Now I hope you two can get it together and start making them babies."

Frank and Mallory looked at each other and burst into laughter. Mick, having put on his grumpy expression, couldn't hold it. He joined in, laughing louder than either of them.

The End

CONTINUE READING...

Thank you for reading **The Mayor's Fiancée** *!* Are you wondering **what to read next?** Why not read **The Nurse Finds Love?** Here's a peek for you:

"No."

Sometimes – more often than not, these days – the word *no* seemed to haunt Adele Cowen. Reading over the terse note once more, she gave a shaky sigh and put a hand to her forehead. No matter how many times she looked over the words, there was no changing their message. Once again, her quest for gainful employment in her chosen field as a nurse had been denied – proven to be futile.

That made six. Six demurrals of varying degrees of politeness, in just the past two months. It wasn't that her education was lacking; she'd gone to nursing college at sixteen and had worked in a military hospital for three years after her graduation. And she knew in her heart it wasn't because her qualifications, both ethical and official, weren't up to snuff. After all, in the four years in total she had worked as a nurse, she had developed a reputation for her kindness, her soft touch, her grace under fire.

And she knew, each time she applied for work, it was impossible that the prospective employer could miss how she wore her heart on her sleeve when it came to her vocation. Adele loved people, and there was nothing she wanted more than to take care of them, to help out wherever she could.

It was ironic, now that she thought of it. In the end, it was that desperation to be of use, to fix and save the wounded, that likely kept her from being employed right now. And it was all due to Gerald Foster.

Once more, she heaved a sigh at the thought of his name. How strange to think that his name had once thrilled her to the core, filling her with the hope of a romantic future, of being loved and cared for. Now there was nothing left of her dreams but dust and ashes – and a persistent inability to find work.

She could not put all the blame at Gerald's door. She herself must bear some of it. After all, despite her strong moral upbringing, she had allowed him to persuade her that their engagement was as good as marriage, that they should start their lives together as man and wife before the ring was on her finger, before their vows were properly exchanged. She couldn't help but writhe in embarrassment and shame at the very thought of it. At least, she reminded herself, she'd the moral fortitude to insist they keep to their separate bedrooms; although at times, she felt as though she had been persuaded in so many other ways that the simple act of denying him a shared bed meant nothing in the face of the facts.

Visit HERE To Read More!

https://ticahousepublishing.com/mail-order-brides.html

THANKS FOR READING!

If you **love Mail Order Bride Romance, <u>Visit Here</u>**

https://wesrom.subscribemenow.com/

to find out about all **<u>New Susannah Calloway Romance Releases!</u> We will let you know as soon as they become available!**

If you enjoyed *The Mayor's Fiancée,* would you kindly take a couple minutes to leave a positive review on Amazon? It only takes a moment, and positive reviews truly make a difference. Thank you so much! I appreciate it!

Turn the page to discover more Mail Order Bride Romances just for you!

ABOUT THE AUTHOR

Susannah has always been intrigued with the Western movement - prairie days, mail-order brides, the gold rush, frontier life! As a writer, she's excited to combine her love of story with her love of all that is Western. Presently, Susannah lives in Wyoming with her hubby and their three amazing children.

www.ticahousepublishing.com
contact@ticahousepublishing.com

www.ingramcontent.com/pod-product-compliance
Lightning Source LLC
Chambersburg PA
CBHW071917120726
48001CB00005B/1770